A black eyed kid is living in Gavin and Drew Mason's bedroom. Will their deadly secret be discovered?

A BLACK EYED KID COMES TO STAY

ZAROK AND THE DOGS OF HELL

K.M AKEHURST

ACORN

Many thanks to Erik Stormtrooper
for his amazing font.

Many thanks to Acorn for all their work in the production
of this Young Adult title. And special thanks to Leila.
Thanks to designer, Ravina Patel for her work
to bring my cover together.

TABLE OF CONTENTS

CHAPTER ONE
FIREWORK NIGHT

Gavin, who was eleven, had been sent to his bedroom along with his younger brother Drew. His sister Billie, who was just seven, had voluntarily joined them. 'Now I know what jail feels like!' groaned Gavin.

'It wouldn't be so bad. I mean, us hanging out in our rooms like what we usually do, but it's Fireworks Night!' exclaimed Drew bitterly.

'I hate dad!' declared Gavin passionately, whilst picking a large hole in the knee of his jeans. 'I hate him more!' agreed Drew, taking an imaginary swing at his boxing apparatus.

'I don't!' disagreed a wide-eyed Billie. 'He's a nice dad, and mummy took me to see the fireworks in the park with Abjola. It started at half past six and the fireworks were lovely! It's a shame that you missed them– they were soo pretty!'

'Pretty?!' articulated Gavin in mock horror. 'We don't want to go to the fireworks coz they're pretty!' But Drew said shyly, 'Well I do. You got to admit they are pretty and with zany colours too! I like 'em when they all go off together at once like a purple fountain,' he added poetically.

'Yes, but we don't go to the fireworks for that? It's Guy Fawkes! Guy Fawkes Night!' protested Gavin. 'He used to live long ago and was a rebel, and later on, they light a massive bonfire an' we get to eat loads of hot potatoes with no knives and forks or any of that. Anyway, he was a rebel of the highest order coz he tried to blow up the Houses of Parliament! He's an anti-hero, like one of us, and we gotta remember him! Remember, remember the fifth of November…' he muttered mysteriously under his breath.

'What does that mean?' asked Billie in a clear, bell-like voice. She had settled comfortably on the boy's thick shag pile rug and rolled herself up in it.

'It means that you are a 'goodie-two-shoes' and that's why you got to go to the fireworks an' we didn't!'

Billie hesitated a moment before asking, 'Why didn't you want to go to the fireworks?' Gavin turned on her incredulously.

'Want?! It's not a case of *want!* It's *dad*, isn't it! He keeps trying to ruin my life!'

'Yeah, he's banished us to our room, hasn't he,' Drew helpfully explained to his sister (as if addressing no one in particular.)

'That's right! He makes me miss the fireworks just coz of the stupid hand grenade thing. Just because I was tryin' to be helpful to 'em finding old hand grenades from the war buried in the garden. How was I supposed to know they were potatoes mum had planted, what with all them wiry bits sticking out n' everything?! And it wasn't actually my fault I lobbed one at the neighbour. I didn't mean to hit him – he just got in the way!' Gavin slapped his brother on the back sympathetically.

'I know what you mean Drew. Just coz of a stupid old potato!' Gavin continued with his story.

'Mine's even worse. He's stopped me going just because I borrowed his mobile phone to call a couple of mates or so.' He furrowed his brow, lost in thought.

'Didn't you drop it into the pond though Gav?' asked Drew. Billie was listening intently, becoming more sorry for them as they went on.

'No? It *fell* in the pond! And then I tried to mend it for him. I heard that if you put it in a bowl of rice it mends it, but how did I know the rice was supposed to be bone dry!' Drew realised what must have happened.

'You put it in that cooked yellow rice from the other day then. Ha ha! Dipstick!' Drew laughed, and the boys had a quick tussle to resolve it.

'Anyway, his mobile phone is rubbish,' said Gavin. 'It's practically a brick phone compared to mine!'

Drew agreed saying, 'I get that, when he nicked your mobile phone last week!' Gavin paused before answering, 'Weell… He confiscated it, but I've not had it back for weeks. It's not fair!'

Billie's mouth widened. 'Um, that's stealing!' she acknowledged.

'Exactly Billie. That's what we're trying to tell you. Dad's a thief! He's wronged us! And his is a rubbish phone and mine's brilliant. He wants to use my one for himself! He's stopped me from meeting the Dogs of Hell down at the recreation ground tonight, on Guy Fawkes Night too, all coz of that!'

'Shh… Dogs of Hell's a secret, Gav. We don't want Billie hearing about that.' But Billie knew already.

'I know you got a top secret club called the Dogs of Hell!' enlightened Billie, looking a tad excited. Drew saw that he needed to ward her off of the subject.

'You know what Gav, I'm a bit sick of the Dogs of Hell. It seems a bit babyish now that we're nearly grown up. I think we should set up a more military operation. At least we could call it 'The Dudes of Hull' or something.' Billie looked a little less gratified by that. 'Go n' get us some biscuits Bill, I'm starving!'

'It's stealing from the biscuit tin,' replied Billie evenly.

'No it isn't. Those biscuits belong to the person who made 'em!' plumped Drew righteously. Dutifully, Billie soon came back with the whole contents of the biscuit tin. The three of them now sat in a triangle on the floor, munching one biscuit after the other, before licking the chocolate off the top first. Now Drew remembered something.

'You know what I saw today!' he announced confidentially. 'I saw dad going into the betting shop at lunchtime!'

'That's called the bookies!' clarified Gavin looking interested.

'Alright, the bookies then. Anyhow, my teacher Mr Jackson once said that betting shops were vices of evil! He said that there were too many in one street and other shops, like grocers, should be there instead. He said they were a dark force on the face of consumerism.'

'What's conzumerzm? questioned Billie,' looking shocked. (Gavin ignored her.)

'I knew it! That means dad must be possessed by a dark force... Forces of evil!' added Gavin, his face now assuming the look of a detective working on a case.

'D'ya know what I know though...' Drew continued. 'The way Jackson explained it, was that if you go into a betting shop, you put a coin in the machine or place a bet, and then they take your money. You try to get it back by putting more in, and then they take that as well! It goes on until they got every last penny. But then, when they find out you've got no more money for them, they come round n' try and take your house!' Drew paused to glare importantly at his audience. Billie looked as if she were about to cry, but Drew had more.

'Yeah?! Go on Drew,' urged his brother impressed.

'Er, well then they sort of take your car as well.'

'What else?' cried Billie pulling at her braided hair.

'Well, they take the lawnmower. Anything they can get their hands on really.'

'Do they take any of our nice things? Will they take dressing up clothes?' asked a red-eyed Billie, her alarm increasing.

'Yes they do! Like they'd take them expensive shoes mum's got with red soles, and the telly. In the end, you got nothing and have to go and live in a bus stop!'

Billie now burst into tears, big baubles of water running down her sweet face; the watery pearls clinging to her skin.

'Don't worry, Bill!' exclaimed Drew affectionately, putting his arm around his sister. 'We'll look after you!'

'Yeah, it's not happened *yet* Billie. We just gotta let you know what dad's like!'

'I'm going to go to mum now,' she sniffed, blowing her nose on her hair.

'No, don't Bill!' cried Drew.

'You got to stay now!' ordered Gavin firmly. 'You're supposed to be in bed anyway.' That was true, the little girl remembered. She was getting sleepy...

'All I'm saying is that we gotta watch dad! He's been taken by the grip of... evil...' finished Drew grimly.

'It's not completely his fault he's got to give all our money away...' confirmed Gavin. He now took out his drum and got a beat going, followed by a magnificent drum roll. The rhythm was quite soothing. Drew joined in, slapping out a complimentary rhythm on his knees.

'It explains why he took my phone –maybe to sell it as rogue trade. And it explains why he wouldn't let us go to go and see Guy Fawkes, as he didn't have any pocket money to give us. He couldn't afford it!' realised Drew, now seeing his dad in a completely different light – as a man who had fallen on hard times and was now struggling to meet his oppressor's demands. 'I like Mr Jackson, he's really nice for a teacher and I believe him. And I bet if he was our dad, he wouldn't treat us so terribly,' added Drew, as if that had settled matters.

'Never mind all that now! What are the Dogs of H…, I mean, the Happy Dudes (he now changed the name entirely for Billie's benefit), going to think of me as their supreme leader when I fail to turn up for our 'Calls of Duty' down the Recreation Ground tonight?'

'You could just go out the window or the back door!' protested Billie, who now felt crestfallen and sad for her brother's sake.

'Too late innit!' scowled Gavin. 'Bet it's all over now!'

'Couldn't we see some fireworks; like some late ones from our window?' suggested Drew, who was scanning the view outside their bedroom window hopefully.

'Yes, let's!' cried out Billie, more cheerful now. 'We can hear bangs. Bang! Bang! There goes one now!' The three of them stood in front of the bedroom window now, noses pressed against the glass.

'It's no good,' said Gavin mournfully. 'We c'n hear 'em but we can't see em!

The tree's in the way for one, and it's a bit misty.' Drew now stood on a chair, stretching his neck, his face extended upwards.

'It's the same view,' he reported even more mournfully. 'Just pink and green light in the clouds where fireworks are exploding underneath!'

'Ooohh… Pink and green coloured lights!' cried Billie. 'Another Bang! Pop!' she squealed.

'Pink lights are nothing Billie!' scolded Gavin. 'We can't *see* any blinkin' fireworks!'

'Oh! You said a rude word!' scolded Billie back.

'No, it ain't!' said Gavin. 'I know tons of ruder words than that!'

'Shup!' warned Drew. 'She'll tell mum.' As if on cue, their mum called upstairs.

'Are you alright boys?' she yelled anxiously.

'No, we are not!' shouted back Drew hotly. Their mum, Miriam, concluded from that response they *were* alright. *Mind you,* she considered, *had Brian been a bit harsh on them?* Still, they had all passed a fantastic Halloween. She would say nothing now and take it up with their dad later.

The boys had a nice large bedroom. It was painted in blue and dark green, but the paintwork was almost totally obscured by posters. The boys had allocated themselves the two sides of the room. When they fell out, they created strict divisions using masking tape, so that the other could not cross over to their side. If one of them did, fighting ensued. So they had a long bamboo stick, extricated from the garden, which enabled them to 'pole vault' to the door, as they put it. Except in the main, they got on really well and were great buddies. A quick fight usually sorted things out. Many of the posters gracing their walls were of their favourite band: Monster Metallions. Both Gavin and Drew were very proud of their poster collection they had built up over the years.

Their bedroom window looked out onto a decent garden, which they appreciated a lot as they didn't use to have one. They liked to spend time out there and make things in the sizeable shed. Sometimes, they liked to hang out there playing music too as it was certainly roomy enough.

They lived in quite a nice neighbourhood, having moved from the capital's suburbs. Well, their parents thought it was nice enough, but the boys called it 'the most boring place in the universe'. The town they lived in was called Higglesdon Wick.

Drew had now taken up one of his favourite pastimes to amuse his brother and sister. It was pulling faces. He practised his latest faces in the mirror first, before clowning around and showing them off.

'This one's called 'The Vampire', he revealed, setting off Gavin guffawing loudly.

'And this one's called 'dad-in-a-mood!' drawled Drew, swinging round to face them, his face contorted into a ghastly mould (not unlike 'The Vampire'.) Gavin was now in stitches rolling on the floor. Drew turned back to the mirror, pulling a few different faces in quick succession, putting his fingers either side of his mouth and stretching his jaw as far as it would go. Then he changed his mind, and pulled at his eyelids to reveal an eye white, whilst emitting a blood-curdling moan at Billie.

'Aaarghh!' she yelped. 'Oh, oh!' she cried, burying her head in her brother's shoulder.

'Get off!' he issued, pushing her away so that she fell on the bed. The three of them goofed around then, laughing happily. It was such a nice atmosphere now. The lights were low, and still the violet-pink lights could be seen flickering outside, colouring the bedroom walls every now and again. The room colour now reverted to blue, yet a really bright, electric blue. That was awesome!

'Gosh, that was a good one!' yelled Gavin. 'No bangs, but how bright was that?!'

'That looked more yellowish, I mean whitish, than they do with the main bedroom light on!' exclaimed Gavin as the colour changed.

'Or even daylight!' added Drew. 'Crikey! We can just imagine what they are like! I bet that one was a Catherine wheel!'

'I bet that one was a Ferris wheel!'

'Out! There's no such one!'

'We c'n have our own 'Rave Club' in a minute at this rate!' Gavin ventured.

The bedroom waxed from pink again into a blinding white with blue strobes. The three children cried, 'Wow!', 'Wha-haay!' whilst taking in each other's brightly lit faces. They blinked wildly before screwing up their eyes completely. Billie then held her hand to her head as if shading it from the sun.

'That was soo cool!' laughed Drew, turning back to the mirror to resume his *repertoire* of 'faces' and impressions. But just then, something made him hesitate... *Wh...what?! What was this...?* Drew's elastic face froze. *There-was-a-face-in-the-mirror-that-wasn't-his-own!* Drew ducked, placing his own *visage* to the side of the mirror to make sure the face definitely wasn't his! The face went. *Had he been seeing double?* His brain tried to process this as he swirled around, open mouthed, to face his brother. He couldn't say anything... *Cripes...*thought Drew.

He looked back in the mirror, then checked himself, before returning to peeping into the glass from the side. *The face was back!* Unmistakably, a kid's face was gazing motionlessly at him! You couldn't detect his eyes very well as he was wearing a black hoodie. The blood froze in Drew's veins. His senses were kicking in. The face continued to gaze, though it now began to fade, bedecked in coloured mists, before coming back… In and out of the mists it came. *It was no illusion,* decided Drew. No illusion, as it kept coming back, and was now more constant and solid than ever!

Drew swept round to face Gavin, while feeling the eyes of the ghostly visage boring into his back.

'Er… Er Gav…' he said, almost in a whisper. 'You didn't invite Reubin round, did ya?'

'No. Why?!' Gavin was eyeing him curiously.

'Well… It's just I saw a face in the mirror. Might it be him?'

'Is it his face?'

'No. Dunno! He's wearin' a hoodie as usual?' Drew decided hopefully.

'You're jokin' aren't you? Don't do bad jokes bruv!'

Intrigued, Gavin made his way back to the bedroom window, scraping his heel across the floor, and threw open the sash as wide as possible. There was a flat rooftop below, where the kitchen was. The drainpipes outside their bedroom and alongside the kitchen wall made for an easy entry and exit (when there were no parents around.)

'Pssst! Reubin! Are you out there?!' hissed Gavin loudly.

'Oi Reubin! Up 'ere! Don't play jokes man!'

Reubin was Gavin's best friend in his year at school and also happened to live close by. He almost lived at the Masons' family home at times. But Gavin felt a knot inside. Instinctively, he knew it was not Reubin!

'Gav, Gav… Come here!' urged Drew in a throaty whisper, pulling his brother over, so he was beside him by the mirror.

Gavin inclined his ear to Drew, who said in a throaty whisper (making Gavin's ear wet with spittle), 'Shhh! Don't tell Billie… Get her out of here will you, but there's a lad in the mirror?!' Gavin turned to face the mirror. Sure enough, there was indeed a lad in the mirror! Eerily, his face was surrounded by coloured lights. Shocked, Gavin turned away and then looked back again. It was still there… He took a double take… *No way. It definitely wasn't Reubin!*

'Er… Billie,' he started, his voice quaking a bit.

'I think…er… I sort of think you ought to get to bed now and…' But it was too late. Billie had seen it!

'Aarghhh!!' she screamed. 'Oh, oh! Oh! Ohhhh!!!'

'It's alright Billie, it's alright! It's just Reubin dressed up. He's still dressed up from Halloween like! I mean Guy Fawkes! Just get to bed alright? Drew will come in a minute and read you a story and tuck you in, OK?!'

'Yeah! I'll bring you a hot chocolate Billie, OK? Be with you in a minute!'

'A-a-a f-f-f face!' wailed Billie, shaking. 'I saw a horrid f-f-f face in the bedroom m-mirror!'

'I know Billie. I know, it was Reubin! He didn't know you was in here, did he?'

Billie left their bedroom blubbering; the shock gradually subsiding with her brothers mollifying comments. She fled to her room and waited on Drew to fulfil his promise. The boys gaped at each other aghast. Standing right back now, they both glared at the mirror. The face was back, grinning at them from ear to ear… And what's more, that face did not look wholly human!

'Maybe it's Guy Fawkes himself, come back to visit us from his fiery grave!' guessed Drew, looking at his brother for affirmation. But Gavin replied with a Drew-style, elasticated mouth that stretched over his teeth, which meant *'struth!' What were they going to do now?!*

***

'I'm home, love!' Brian called out to his wife. The boys' mum came running into the kitchen wearing an autumn shawl. 'You're a bit late back from work aren't you?' she said.

'I know,' the children's dad answered, 'but at least we got away from the rat race somewhat, so I don't have to travel back anymore!'

'True!' Miriam replied. 'Did you have a good day in town then?'

'Yeeess… Much the same as usual. I stopped off at the village pub actually to meet Mike. Called you from there, but you must have been at the fireworks. We stayed on, but the shop was open late, so I popped in to get Alex's monthly tech magazine, and I got you some pastries!'

'Oh, that was kind' Miriam replied. 'My favourites,' she approved, opening the brown paper bag. 'Anything else?'

'When we sit down,' he replied kissing her. 'I'm starving. Oh, by the way, I saw our Drew in my lunch break. Hope he wasn't bunking off, but he was walking along with a lass. I think he has a glad eye for her! Anyway, I didn't want to embarrass him. I was about to walk right into them. It's probably his first girlfriend, if it is one yet, so I took a sharp left and dived into the betting shop.' Miriam chuckled smiling. 'Go on?'

'Nothing really. I felt a bit of a twerp in there, so now I had to place a bet! I put one on the football for Geoff at the office. Just a quid or something for a bit of fun; you know, what with the big match happening in our town and that.'

***

CHAPTER TWO
THE MASON FAMILY AND A NEW VISITOR

The Mason family lived at number twenty-four Cherry Tree Lane. They were an ordinary family, which in a way made them extraordinary. Life was pleasant enough for them and also ordinary. Nothing too much out of the ordinary ever happened. They took a holiday or two each year, usually in Ireland to visit family. The children's mum, Miriam, worked as a hairdresser and their Dad, Brian, worked at an office in town. Higglesdon Wick was a small town with a villagey feel to it. There was an old and new part and the boy's school was in the new part of town. Miriam and Brian had two more children that were older than Billie, Gavin and Drew. There had never been any leading lights in the family, but their older sister Frayre, who was fifteen, was proving to be very talented. She lived away from home in term time, having won a scholarship to a performing arts school. Frayre had the attic room upstairs, which the boys were rather envious of since they were not allowed to use it, even when their sister was away.

Then there was Alex. He was fourteen and a half, and rather kept himself to himself, holed up in his room playing computer games and engaging in what Drew and Gavin called 'geeky things'. He was a quiet boy, who unlike Gavin and Drew, liked homework and studied beyond what was uniformly set for him.

Drew would say, 'I can't understand it!' or 'I don't know how he can stand it! He's not that much older than us and he's no fun!' Nevertheless, Gavin and Drew were extremely impressed by Alex's bedroom. It was full of gadgets and lights, set off by an assortment of trendy furniture that he had either sourced or made himself. He pretty much ignored Drew and Gavin except to make scathing comments or play dad to them at times. He was the only one in the family that didn't have red hair.

The Masons had inherited the redheaded gene from their mum's side of the family. Drew was in possession of a head of vibrant hair, which was a handsome shade of red indeed. Gavin's was a more mahogany colour. He found it most unruly (it was just curly), so he liked to keep it as short as possible. Billie was a strawberry blonde with large hazel eyes. Frayre hated her own flame locks and dyed them traffic light red or purple in defiance. None of the children, except for Frayre, were too interested in looks or fashion, apart from wearing sneakers or following made-up fads that caught on at school. They stood out for other reasons though; being a big family in a close community, the Mason's home was a busy one with friends and neighbours making themselves at home there too. As we know, Gavin's best friend Reubin was always round. He had roots in the Caribbean. Gavin found Reubin's heritage interesting although it was not the reason they were best mates. Reubin wished that his mum wasn't such friends with Miriam, as the two would gossip about their boys and find them out.

Reubin and Gavin became schoolmates when the Masons first moved to Higglesdon Wick, which introduced Miriam to Reubin's mum, Honour. The two mums quickly found out they got on very well, sharing interests like dog walking, the local choir and 'around the world cuisine'. They also took more of an interest in each other's traditions.

The locale of Higglesdon Wick enjoyed the benefits and introductions that a well-integrated small town brought and Gavin and Reubin's school was a multi-cultural one. So it was normal for them to have friends of colour, including from different backgrounds and cultures.

Gavin and Reubin didn't give much thought about how different they looked to each other. With your typical playground mix of children, it was no issue for them. They were just proud to get on with each other. It was the ideals of their club that mattered to them; which had nothing to do with society's values, to say the least. It would be fair to say they were fortunate to have been brought up without racial prejudice. The children were aware of this and their school was hot on equal opportunities and took diversity seriously. It made Higglesdon Wick work well. Naturally, things weren't harmonious for everyone in the neighbourhood, and with an exclusive independent school in close proximity, class war was often just around the corner.

Drew's best mates were Gregory and Terry, of which Greg visited the Masons the most. He was mixed race, being half-Ghanaian and half-Scottish. Handsome and bright he was too. Terry was fair with sandy hair and a dry sense of humour. He had some Welsh in his background, although he was born in Higglesdon Wick. The two lads were cheeky so and so's and a bit of a double act, as well as besties.

Greg and Reubin lived in King Charles Street; a stone's throw from them. Usually, the boys would meet up before school or *en route*. They either walked to school if they spent all their bus fare on sweets, or caught the bus together. Drew's and Gavin's other buddies were Raj, who was a rather sweet, self-effacing Indian boy. Then there was Lee, who lived further away from them and attended Higglesdon Wick Secondary School. Lee, who was Chinese, was the more sensible of the bunch in what was a pretty 'full on' band of buddies. Lee hated being asked, 'But where do you really come from?'

They all felt – and were – equally British, having all been brought up in England. Drew and his friends (who felt far too grown up for their age to still be in Juniors) could not wait to join Gavin and Reubin at Higglesdon Wick Secondary School. The boys would sometimes sneak into each other's side of the school to meet up, or would get together for pranks. Yes, indeed, there were lots of friends and neighbours around them. *But just who was our friend reflected in the mirror that night? And was he a friend at all?!*

'Not Reubin, was it?!' enquired Drew of his brother, without any conviction whatsoever in his voice.

'No!' came back Gavin irritably. But he was not really annoyed with Drew. He just got like that when he was flummoxed.

'Who was it then?' asked Drew matter of factly.

'Look, how should I know?! Let's wait for him t' show up again, aye?' Gavin suggested bravely, even though he was frankly terrified. Billie had fallen straight to sleep, which was just as well. It was about 10.30pm now and the boys should have turned in too by now. Instead, the boys waited, switching their gaze from the mirror to the window alternately, while counting the minutes. Then, like a light switching on, the room was suddenly bathed in phosphorescent white light!

'Crikey!' murmured Gavin. 'It's some dude!'

'Crikey!' whispered Drew, echoing his brother.

The shape in the mirror moved, while the sash on their bedroom window creaked and inched up. Unable to bear any more suspense, and perhaps foolishly, the boys hurled themselves towards the window and threw up the sash properly. They saw one glimpse of a deathly, pinched white face, gaping at them from under an oversized hoodie, before 'the dude', in one sprightly action, clambered in! Gavin and Drew stood back cautiously, staring in disbelief at the ghostly encounter who had now stationed himself on the window-sill, cross-legged and looking down.

'Crikey!' burst out Gavin again, looking wildly at Drew. 'He's in our room bruv! What do we say to him?!' There was an awkward silence, then…

'Um! Ummm… Hello!' greeted Drew brightly, at last finding his voice.

'Hi!' drawled 'the dude', still not looking up. He had an American accent.

'We can communicate with him…' hissed Gavin to Drew. Now Gavin ventured to address the dude as best he could.

'Er… We had thought you might be the ghost of Guy Fawkes! But you're not are you?' surmised Gavin bending his head, trying to get a look at the dude.

'Guy Forx, man?' Sorry! I don't know what you mean', replied the uninvited guest. He seemed a bit shifty. Then he swung his legs right round.

'He's polite,' whispered Drew to Gavin. 'He's not being funny!'

'Hello mate!' greeted Drew again, offering a hand.

'Hi! We've had that conversation already!' insisted the dude, finally looking up at his two flabbergasted hosts. The dude had white translucent skin and his tiny mouth was like a slit in his face. His eyes were enormous, dewy, black and opaque.

'It doesn't take Einstein to work out he ain't human!' whispered Gavin hoarsely, trying to catch his breath, as he was of course, in a mild state of shock. Drew was too. The boy was quivering now, open-mouthed.

'Shut the window for gawdsake!' said Gavin, pretending they were suffering from the cold. (That was his way of asking the dude in.) The dude was gazing remotely at them now, almost sadly. Then, unexpectedly, he managed a sweet little smile. The boys laughed, relaxing immediately. All the tension was taken out of the cold air, and the picture changed. Drew and Gavin could now see a young boy, or teen, of the same age in front of them.

'Aw, you are quite nice, are you alright?' tried Drew.

'Not really dude,' replied the dude, looking glum.

'What's happened then? And why did you 'weird us out' in our mirror and want to come in?!' asked Gavin bluntly.

'And why were you grinning from ear to ear… That really freaked me out!' added Drew, forgetting to keep his voice down. The dude faced them both squarely and seriously. The brothers glanced down, noticing he was wearing trakkie bottoms to match his hoodie. Evenso, it was obvious the dude was as thin as a rake. They took in his hands. They were also appallingly thin and tapering, added to which he had six fingers– not five. Drew suppressed a gasp.

'I'm here because I need a friend and it was a way of getting your attention,' explained the dude. 'I saw you making faces, and hell, I like jokes too. I mean, seeing you all playing cheered me up!' He paused for a moment.

'I've come a long way…' he sighed.

'Is that all?' Drew asked the intruder. 'Why us? Just because we are up late?'

'Yes! Well, not exactly. It's true that the other windows were dark with the blinds drawn, but I landed in your garden…' Gavin continued staring at the intruder, processing what he had just said and remembering all the coloured lights…

'You speak American, which means you're a Yank. Can you teach me American?' enthused Gavin.

'Sure dude!' agreed the dude heartily.

'I wanna learn American too!' demanded Drew, wanting a piece of the action. You say 'to-may-tow' and not 'tomato!' don't you!'

'Tomatoes?' repeated the dude confused.

'You say don't *chya*', not 'don't *you*', insisted Gavin. 'I know 'cause I perfect my American when I hit the sweet shops in the areas they don't know me. They think I'm from Miami!' he revealed. The dude chuckled softly before saying, 'I take it ya mean tomatoes is food. I don't really like, well, eat, tomatoes.'

'No?' I don't mean in a boring salad. I mean pizza. You must like pizza! My favourite is pepperoni and Drew's is Hawaiian, with pineapple and ham! All Americans must like pizza as it comes from there… and Italy,' Gavin added uncertainly.

'I'm afraid not!' replied the dude, picking at his shoelace nervously. The boys noticed he had a tiny, pinched nose, with very small yet prominent nostrils. They were trying not to let his odd appearance stand in the way of what promised to be a highly entertaining guest.

'My favourite food… And the food I have to eat,' stated the dude, 'is molasses, a mix of vinegar castor oil and soda, and gourds or sweet potato… Best is cactus! Even that isn't my real diet, but it suffices.'

'Whoa! Whadya mean suffices, man?' cried Gavin, launching into his best 'American' to try and make 'the dude' feel at home. 'I sure as hell dunno any of that stuff, crazy cat!' he finished, getting into his stride.

'That was awful! *Embarrassing!*' Drew told his brother with a withering expression.

'The dude will think you are taking the mickey out of him,' added Drew, twisting his baseball cap so that it sat backwards on his head.

'You're not really from here at all, are you?' Drew addressed the dude sedately, knowing in his gut what was coming. He was a well brought up boy and found it difficult to ask him outright.

'You mean you wanna know if I'm an alien, Drew? Yeah! OK, I get you. The rap is, I ain't from these parts, and I'm not really from America either. That's right! You have me! You guys have gotta know sometime that I'm an alien alright!' (It seemed the dude was happy that he didn't have to pretend.)

For some reason, although it was not funny, the three of them fell about laughing. Such an absurd situation called for such a response to lighten the atmosphere in what was, after all, a groundbreaking moment! It wasn't really a revelation though. His arrival alone had made it pretty obvious that he was undoubtedly an alien! Boys are boys and they had different ways of tackling something as heavy-duty as this. Heavy information as it was, they weren't going to weigh it up as such. Drew and Gavin's answer was immediate, and to them, obvious –the alien had to stay! But Gavin's and Drew's unrestrained voices and occasional whoop had proved too much for someone. The door burst open, whereupon their older brother Alex stood there framing it, his face red with fury.

'Could you make a bit more noise, please? I haven't quite finished my physics homework yet!' he spat. His eye then turned to the dark figure at the foot of the window. The dude's head was face down, with his hood characteristically obscuring his face. Drew had acted quickly, chucking some junk, including old gear and stockings stuffed with conkers, over their alien guest.

'I don't think much of your Guy Fawkes effort!' sneered Alex. 'You didn't fatten it up properly. You need to stuff the gear inside 'The Guy', not just sling it over the thing willy-nilly! Mind you, I don't s'pose it matters how rubbish it looks, as you weren't allowed to go! Good thing too! I bet you'd have created some kind of trouble. Now if you don't mind, could the pair of you just GET TO BED!' yelled Alex, making his exit with a slam of their door. Luckily, the room was dark now with just a small bedroom light on beside Drew's bed.

'Yes dad, I mean Alex,' said Drew meekly (and sarcastically) when he'd gone.

'Phew that was lucky!' breathed Gavin. 'Look, we need to stay up a bit more, find out about you dude. But we gotta be quiet, OK?!'

'It's you that's makin' all the noise,' complained Drew. Gavin plucked some mouldy looking hotdogs from under the bed that had been extracted, presumably unwanted, from the school canteen, and out came two cans of fizzy orange for the boys to share.

'Right,' said Gavin. 'Let's have a midnight feast. We need to find out the burning question! Should we let what's-his-name be in the Dogs of Hell or what?' Although Gavin was not really getting his priorities right, in his own mind, their alien guest had already signed up to stay with them. Drew also assumed that the alien would be staying too. It hardly needed clarifying, but Drew said, just in case, 'You are staying, right?'

'Yeah!' replied the alien simply. 'If you are sure it's OK?'

'Do you wanna join the Dogs of Hell?' Gavin asked the alien earnestly.

'Very much so!' replied the alien dude, relaxing again now.

'You have to swear an oath of allegiance,' put in Drew swiftly. 'Not today, right now, but soon, when you meet the others…' But now the boys paused for thought. *The reality of the situation… How were they going to get 'him' out and about?* Gavin suddenly came back down to earth. Some practicalities were in order.

'Have you got a name? What's your name?' asked Gavin, who was kneeling opposite the alien, his mouth crammed full of hotdog.

'It's Varoqswovianphyzn-oskz-Bzerzhithsperothzhargoidn-tkt TarknZaerokc!' replied the alien in an incomprehensible gabble. (It sounded something like that anyway…)

'We can't call you that!' cried Drew. 'What about your nickname?' The dude looked at a loss.

'I don't know that I really like that name,' mused Drew doubtfully, shaking his head. 'Can we call you a name that we've made up?'

'Shh…Don't Drew, it's rude!' There was an awkward silence.

'I don't mind,' responded the alien dutifully, his large, searching eyes questing.

'Well, we can't call you something ordinary, like John or Peter. It wouldn't suit you! What about the last bit –

Tarknzarokc?' That sounds both American and friendly and cool!'

'No, change the last bit… Zaerokc is better!' corrected Gavin, not wanting his brother to have the last word on such an important matter!

'Zaerkokcn, it is then. I mean Zarok!' confirmed Drew, changing the conversation quickly before his brother could butt in again.

'When you stay here, we will have to move you about. We can't tell our parents, as they might not like you as much as we do. You know, she always moans about extra washing and things. You can stay under Gavin's bed in the corner, the one with the steps up, and we'll clear a space underneath it. Then you can alternate between that and the garden shed.'

'Don't worry Zarok. It's massive, and the ole boy an' ole girl hardly ever go in there. Dad is always planning to do stuff but never gets round to it.'

The boys now stared at their uninvited guest whilst chomping on the remainders of their cold and soggy hotdogs. Just how were they going to put the question of Zarok's appearance to him? Zarok had his head cast down, almost ashamed, having read their faces.

'Don't worry Zarok,' soothed Drew, as if he had read Zarok's thoughts too. 'I've been thinking… You know that you're so pale, and there's no one *that* white, not even in the South Pole, or the North Pole and…'

'There might be in Greenland. In Greenland they are!' disagreed Gavin, for the sake of it.

'How d'you know? You been there lately, have you?' asked Drew.

'Look, his face is see-through, and we can't take him out like that…' pointed out Gavin, talking as if Zarok was no longer in the room.

'So? I've got an idea that'll kill two birds with one stone. My neighbour, Mrs Small, said that means you can have two answers in one!'

'Get on with it then!' said Gavin irritably.

'My sister's got a stupid tanning booth in her room. It makes your skin colour change to orange. You gotta spray yourself about six times. So if you go out, people won't guess you are an alien!' finished Drew tactlessly. Tact was neither of the brothers' strong points.

'What about the other things?' remarked Gavin, wincing at Zarok's oversized opaque dark eyes that now glowed with a violet lustre. Drew ignored this.

'We can use her room as an emergency den if there is any trouble over keeping him in the shed or our room,' explained Drew, his face centred on the alien's, trying to keep up his spirits.

'More like the tanning booth in an emergency too!' said Gavin, cupping his head in his hands.

'Can't you see that we can't take him out?! We'll have to keep him under the bed and in the shed all the while he stays, or, or…'

'Do I get a say in this dudes?' asked the alien suddenly, straightening up.

'Er… Yep…? Go on. Go for it!' said Drew a bit relieved.

'I think I might have to go out sometimes. Maybe at night… I'll need to stretch my legs and get some air in my chest,' he explained, patting his bony upper regions that stuck out a bit below his neckline. He went on…

'At night, folks tend not to pay attention to you. But I don't mind putting your tanning booth to the test if that's what you want.'

'Yeah! OK Zarok! And if we get found out, you'll have to come to school with us, and then we will have to use my sister Frayre's tanning booth crap on you,' agreed Drew, rubbing his brow, suggesting that it was getting a bit hard to think all of this out now.

'If he comes to school with us, he'll need the works, including sunglasses!' observed Gavin. 'And they don't allow sunglasses in school.'

Now to appease his hosts, Zarok tentatively pulled back his hood for the first time. His cranium was slightly globular, sparsely adorned with super fine silver hair. His brow was furrowed and hairline high. His eyebrows were non-existent, and his neck was abnormally long. It was a look that should have made him look very old, but he looked incredibly delicate instead. Instinctively, Drew held out his palm and the alien held his out too. Clutching it, he could tell the alien's thumb was placed higher on his hands than a human's, and Zarok's grip was extra tight. It was no surprise that his wrists were tiny.

'We gotta go to school in the morning Zarok, so me an' Drew's going to wash and get into bed now, then we can chat for a bit in bed. Drew's goin' to sort you out so you're comfy and sheltered, alright?'

'No problem!' affirmed Zarok, hauling himself up, ready to help Drew create a space under Gavin's bed. Once Gavin had cleaned his teeth, which he usually forgot to do accidentally-on-purpose, he snuggled down and soon the boys were all in bed with the light off. The old-fashioned garden street lamp from next door provided a comely luminescence. Light or not, the boys were not in the least bit scared of Zarok.

It was arranged that Zarok would hang out in their bedroom during the day. Any sign of trouble, he would take to his undercover shelter beneath Gavin's bed. Both the boy's parents would be at work, he was assured. But the big question of where Zarok came from, why he was here and where he was going, still hung in the air. They had made his acquaintance over two hours ago and they were still none the wiser! The boys knew they could easily be up all night! Drew was already closing his eyes and falling into a doze. 'I'm totally wide awake!' he said, but Gavin ignored him and whispered down to his new alien friend.

'Hey Zarok?'

'Yes Gavin?'

'I said yer name right, dint I? Yeah! Zarok, you and me are mates now, and Drew is too. Where you from?'

'I'm from a place often called the Devil's Highway, Gavin. Well, not exactly from there, because I'm from another solar system, but that is where we have been staying…'

'DEVIL'S HIGHWAY?!' Drew woke up instantly and sat up in bed with a start.

'*We?* What do you mean *we?* Don't say there's more of you?' yelped Gavin.

'Don't worry. They will not be coming here!' Zarok assured them.

'Let me explain a little. My people, my peers, took me on a joyride this evening. In fact, I was taken on a joyride to Earth in the first place! Come to think of it, maybe they knew there would be lots of fireworks going off in England tonight. It doesn't take us long to fly here in our little craft, Gavin…'

'A UFO! Maad! I bet it was a UFO! That means you came in a *UFO*, and that's why there were mad coloured lights and everything!' yelled Drew. They could now hear resolute footsteps stomping down the corridor and next off, there were three loud knocks at the door!

'Could the pair of you SHUT UP! I got a science exam tomorrow! Now Good B*****'Night!' Alex stamped off.

'Yikes! We'd better hurry up… You and your big mouth Drew!'

Gavin decided to cut to the quick. 'So what are you exactly, Zarok? You don't mind me askin', do you? Like, I know there's aliens out there; like the men in black. I read a thing about the men in black and they come to your door, pretendin' to be humans. But they're not human! Then there are the Vorgavonons out of that film, 'True Star Battles!' They said they were made up, but it was leaked out that some people said they were real! They was real aliens I tell you. Greg told us!'

'I'm what is known here as a 'Black Eyed Kid', Gavin. I will tell you more in due course because you must be tired now. But before you read all about me, I must tell you that I am nothing like a normal 'Black Eyed Kid' –who has a really awful reputation! That is why they simply dropped me off tonight, leaving me stranded in your garden, in another country too… Because I don't want to do bad things to other people, to humans, for kicks! What I really want to do is find a way to get back to my home planet, where good people from my species live. Goodnight Gavin and Drew, and thank you for letting me in and helping me tonight! I can't tell you that enough! You don't know me, but already you treat me as a… whaddya say? A best mate!'

'It's me n' Drew's pleasure innit! We always like helping people, don't we Drew?!'

But Drew merely said dreamily, *'A Black Eyed Kid from the Devil's Highway!'*

***

CHAPTER THREE
GAVIN AND THE DOGS OF HELL

The next morning Gavin and Drew were pretty exhausted! But they dutifully got themselves dressed and ready for school, then wolfed down their breakfasts. Gavin grabbed his schoolbag, which was missing half its books needed for the day, and a cereal bar and apple for his break. Drew was a slowcoach anyway, and checked up on Zarok before he left, making sure it had not all been a dream. He brought him some molasses and a bottle of vinegar, remembering Zarok's preferences. Gavin was already on his way, yelling 'goodbye' to his mum and shutting the door (a bit too hard), whilst noting that Reubin was waiting for him at the bottom of the path of number twenty- four. They greeted each other by ramming into each other, their rucksacks in front of them. Reubin suddenly pulled back, leaving Gavin careering into him at his front gate and nearly buckling it.

'I thought you had come up the drainpipe last night,' Gavin announced to Reubin, not knowing how to start the story, even to his best friend. Reubin ignored him saying, 'You missed the fireworks, Gav! They were wicked! And you didn't even text us. Waste man! We was all at the bonfire waiting for you!' he added miserably, suddenly glaring at Gavin as if he'd utterly betrayed them. But to Gavin, the fireworks stuff seemed ages ago now, what with the arrival of Zarok. He merely said, 'Shall we walk to school this morning, Reubin? I sort of got something to tell you. It's something big like!'

'OK?!' answered Reubin looking bamboozled. Why didn't his friend explain where he'd got to on Fireworks Night, or seem to even care? 'Tell mi, bruv!'

'Oh no!' said Gavin. 'There's Terry n' Greg at the bus stop. I can't tell them about this. We need to dog them out right now. I need to tell you first!'

'Tell us what, Gav? Hi Terry! Wotcha Greg!'

Terry and Greg looked as if they were up to no good, even though they were hanging around waiting for the number 33 under the bus shelter. They grinned at the approach of their friends, backs against the glass.

'Waited for you last night!' reported Terry to Gavin accusingly.

'Well you can wait for Drew now!' answered Gavin. 'He's coming out in a minute alright? Oh! Let's all meet up at the allotments after school. See ya later!' Greg expertly blew a large pink bubble before letting it splat back over his face, by way of acknowledgement.

'See ya then!' Terry called after him. 'That's if you're goin' to even bother like last night!'

But Reubin and Gavin had already walked on together. Gavin now began to tell his friend about the events that had transpired the night before. He started the story rather unbelievably.

'Guess what? An alien from outer space rocked up at our bedroom last night! He eats molasses and weird vegetables and says he came from 'The Devil's Highway!' Gavin gaped at his friend, his wide eyes imploring.

'Tut!' went Reubin, still miffed. 'Bogus!'

'It's a good story, but it's a poor excuse for not turning up last night! You let us all down, Gav! All the Dogs of Hell managed to get there, so why not you? Anyway, it weren't as much fun without you or Drew!'

'Oh that's old now! It weren't my fault anyway. It was dad's. That's just it –the Dogs of Hell! We've got a new member and he's actually *from* Hell! He's from the *Devil's Highway!!*' Gavin now emphasised this by walking backwards in front of Reubin, whose eyes were as wide as could be. He shook his head before assuming a studious expression, taking it all in. As if there was no dispute whether an alien was in the mix or not he said, 'Big tings! How d' ya know he's from a Devil's Highway, Gav?'

'Coz 'e said he was a Black Eyed Kid that came from there!' retorted Gavin with a snort.

'Oh my days…'breathed Reubin. 'A Black Eyed *Kid*? I think I might have heard about them…'

'What d'ya know?' Gavin asked his friend, brandishing his watch. They were dawdling and likely to be late, so they sped up a little bit.

'Um. I don't know anything. I've just heard of 'em that's all,' said Reubin totally unconvincingly. He went on to expound some wisdom of the kind that Gavin feared the most.

'You don't say, you really have an alien, Gav?! Maad! I c'n bleev you! I believe in aliens! It's not the first time people have seen 'em… Last year, in the paper, it was reported that peeps saw lights in their gardens; spooky ones like! It turned out they weren't street lamps or nothing! That was right here in Higglesdon. But you know what? Grown-ups, a) don't like them, and b) don't believe in them! If they catch you hiding him bruv, he will be in even more trouble than you! They'll take him down the cop shop, or even worse, they'll hand him into special government agents! Hear mi!'

This was quite a speech from Reubin. He was so glad he could confide in him. He really seemed to know about all of this, and Gav felt able to trust him completely straightaway. Gavin could feel a weight being lifted from his shoulders because even though it was exciting, it was a huge responsibility! The thought of Zarok at home, under the bed, sent him into a cold sweat. It was a very odd feeling and one that Gavin hadn't had before. He supposed he was a bit scared and on tenterhooks. Gavin filled in all the details to an incredulous and equally excited Reubin. Slouching through the school gates, they came slap bang into the headmaster, Mr Baldwin.

'Shoulders back you two! Stop slouching, hands out of your pockets and get to class! Move it!'

'Baldy!' muttered Gavin to Reubin. Mr Baldwin had the unfortunate disposition of having the name Baldwin and actually being bald. So it was pretty much set in stone that his pupils would be likely to call him Baldy as a nickname. At break, the two boys met up again to discuss the question of Zarok further.

'You'll come round and meet him tonight, right?!' asked Gavin, who had wanted to speak with Reubin alone, not only because he trusted him, but because he needed his advice as to whether he should let their other friends in on it, and how he could do this.

'Reubin! You know Greg n' Terry. They are Drew's mates, and ours too, of course… And then there's Lee and Raj. An', of course, we're all members of the Dogs of Hell…'

'Obviously! Go on!' pressed Reubin, as he looked furtively around the bleak, grey expanse of the outside area. They wished they could use it like their old playground, but as they were new at secondary school, it took some getting used to.

Of course, he was aware that their discourse was a 'top secret' matter too!

'Well? Who out of our mates can we trust with this? One slip and it will be all round the school… Do we care if it gets round the school?' added Gavin, looking to his friend for advice again.

'Whah? Dem live a luu…' he muttered, which meant 'they'd spoil the plan.'

'Yeah, coz your dad will kill you, and they might take Zarok away for good! They might do science experiments on him and then try and send him to Mars or something!' conjectured Reubin, who had a tendency to catastrophize. Nevertheless, it could certainly be a catastrophe if they didn't do this right.

'OK…OK…Greg, yes! He will be alright with some strict instructions. Lee is super-intelligent and will be able to help us and come up with all sorts of ideas. He's quiet too and won't blab!' Reubin, hands in pockets, looked happy with this. He could not wait to see Zarok and felt he had met him already. He suggested feigning illness and taking the day off school to see him, but Gavin said 'no'. He felt nothing different should happen that could arouse suspicion.

'That's just what I thought, Reuboid. Lee is fine and Greg is a bit iffy, but he will be OK. Terry is just a big mouth and funny too…'

'Yeah, Terry's funny, man! He cracks me up!' agreed Reubin.

'But although Terry is actually risky, it'll be no fun if we don't let him in on Zarok. We will delay it a bit, so that he feels like he's missing out on something. Then we will pin him down and swear him to secrecy if he wants to be in on it. By that time he'll be gagging to know, and to get things right!'

'Yeah! He'll agree to play by the rules then. He can wait a bit until we tell him! Crawb up!'

Just then, the bell for the pre-lunch lessons started ringing out.

'Raj?' questioned Gavin, wandering towards the double doors.

'Raj is cool, and I like him lots. But he's so overexcitable don't ya think, Gav? I think he might have a bit of a strict family. Everything is such a big deal to him, man! But for that reason, we can't have him miss out. He is a risk factor, but he is no longer just an honorary member of the Dogs of Hell.'

'Yeah right!' agreed Gavin, looking down a corridor vacant of children.

'Better go. Raj – yes! He's no more risky than Terry. But we gotta give him a drilling. He's way too excitable, isn't he! That makes all of them, doesn't it?'

'Depending how we do it!' yelled Reubin, who had by now dashed down the corridor at the sight of 'Baldy' lolloping towards the double door entrance.

The boys split; Reubin going off for double history, and Gavin for maths followed by geography. Perhaps he would learn something about America in geography... Suddenly, the prospect of a boring lesson interested him instead. He might just listen to it for once if 'Gulpo' spoke about America. (Gulpo was nicknamed thus due to an oversized Adam's apple.) So Gavin tried studying for once.

It was lunchtime and Gavin was hungry. He avoided Reubin, Lee and Raj, who were chatting animatedly with their classmates in a corner of the canteen. Instead, he took a seat opposite Gulpo, who's real name was Mr Anderson.

'Hello Gavin. Did you enjoy the lesson?' asked Mr Anderson, smiling at the boy's freckled face.

'No,' replied Gavin, bluntly but honestly.

'O-Ohh…' stammered Mr Anderson, plunging his spoon into a lurid looking plate of stew.

'It looks like the contents of the Yangtze, doesn't it, Sir?' commented Gavin mischievously.

'Ha ha! Yes indeed it does! I shall remember that one, Gavin,' said Mr Anderson brightening up. Gavin had surprised him.

'I suppose you do know where the Yangtze is Gavin?' tested Mr Anderson.

'Yes Sir. It's in the River Nile.'

'No! The Yangtze is a river in China. I thought you would know that. Sadly, it is rather polluted,' explained the geography teacher.

'I would like Geography much more Sir, if we could learn about landmarks in America,' asserted Gavin.

'Oh? What kind of landmarks?'

'Well, Death Valley and Las Vegas, and the ole' Devil's Highway… an' Area fifty-three,' advanced Gavin carefully. Mr Anderson laughed a little, cocking his head to one side.

'I think you might mean Area 51 Gavin. Do you know anything about it?'

'Not really,' replied Gavin, swilling his stew around to make a whirlpool effect.

'I doubt we will be coming across such topics on our curriculum, Gavin. But you can always do your own research when you come across something that interests you. Las Vegas, of course, is a city known for gambling, right by the Nevada desert.' And with that Mr Anderson stood up. 'You've given me food for thought Gavin,' he said as he swept off in a teacherly fashion.

After school, Gavin crossed Drew's playground, only to bump into his brother mooching along with their sister Billie.

'What are you doing? We're going to meet up with the others at the allotments!' reproached Gavin.

'I've gotta take Billie to her poxy ballet class, haven't I? Or at least drop her off at mum's hairdressers.'

'Well hurry up then! Maybe it's just as well. We don't want her coming back home when we got Zarok to check up on!' Gavin spotted Raj coming up on his bike and quickly alighted it for a backie, before the pair of them wobbled precariously away.

'Keep up Billie!' ordered Drew, who had now decided to step on it. 'I got important things to do.'

'What important things?' she asked sweetly.

'None of your business!' Drew's mind was back at home and how he needed to be back with Zarok. *Gosh! All the things to attend to… Zarok would need feeding, shown where to shower, where the shed was and allsorts!*

'Mummy bought me some nice new pink ballet shoes, Drew,' proclaimed Billie, skipping along.

'Yippee!' scowled Drew. *Typical! His sisters seemed to get everything they wanted, while he and his brother got nothing!* Drew resolved to ask his parents again about the computer he and Gavin needed. The moment they arrived outside his mum's hairdressers, Drew made a break for it, running for the allotments. He needed to make it by 4.00pm.

The allotment where the boys often gathered belonged to none of their families. From their frequent visits, they had learnt that it was left unattended. They were nice plots extending lengthways up an incline and it felt secluded at the top. Outside the broken shed, there were a couple of benches surrounded by garden cane arrangements where runner beans had run. Drew ran along the narrow strip of grass up to the top, even though he was out of breath. Reubin, Gavin, Greg, Terry, Raj and Lee were all there waiting for him.

'About time too!' scolded his brother, who was the leader of this merry crew of Hell Dogs. The boys went from joking around to standing up and forming a ring and swearing: 'Dogs of Hell, never tell!' while flourishing a four-fingered salute to their heads. Having finished, they sat down as Gavin started proceedings by handing them all a plastic bag with a couple of things inside it.

'That's a mouldy ole Jeffersons plastic bag!' stated Terry, unimpressed.

(Jeffersons was their local supermarket branch.) Gavin assumed his most authoritative stance before declaring, 'To you, it might look like an 'ole Jeffersons plastic bag', but to *us*, it is the property of the Dogs of Hell! For that breach of conduct, you will be on litter duty!' And with that, Gavin emptied the bag's contents on the ground before handing it to him.

'That's an order!' he barked at Terry, who looked helplessly around the allotment. There was nothing but leaves around, so he set off on a path down to the bottom of the plot looking crestfallen.

'Good, he's gone! I'm cool with Tez-face, but we need him out of the way a bit. Listen up gang! We got a new visitor come to stay, and he's from America! Me n' Drew would like to introduce him to you a.s.a.p, maybe even tonight!'

The gang looked unmoved. To them, visitors were an inconvenience and a bore. It meant being on your best behaviour and minding them. But maybe this one had perks to it.

'Will any treats come our way? Are they flush?' enquired Greg hopefully.

'They got good stories or good jokes to tell? We can't let *anyone* into the club!' responded Greg forcefully. 'Specially not older peeps and no family members either!' He made the motion of being sick.

'No! This one's different – very! But listen up everyone. You gotta keep him a secret! Noone can know about him! You all gotta swear an extra oath of allegiance right now!'

They all raised their arms, pressing their hands together, and vowed:

'We swear an oath of allegiance to the club!'

'Top secret!' commanded Gavin. Reubin, who was in the know, gritted his teeth.

'Top secret!' They all repeated and followed suit now, slapping their hands in a hi-five gesture. The club members were looking fired up now.

'Especially you Raj! You can get over excitable and you gotta keep it together on this one!'

'Aw, come on!' he replied indignantly.

Terry came running up the bank panting with the bag full of leaves. Gavin grabbed it, and handed him another bag.

'Your litter duty ain't over yet, Terry mate. Fill up all of them!' Terry grimaced, grabbing the bags and running off, half thinking of splitting.

'Why can't Terry know?' asked Lee blinking.

'He can, but not yet. He needs to know this is a serious matter. He needs to be begging to learn about it, and that means he'll keep it secret better!' explained Gavin, nervously pulling up the grass.

'I vote, you all come round ours tonight at half eight. We'll let you in the backdoor, but you got to be quiet! And when you meet him, you mustn't all go mad! We don't want no 'mad' Dogs of Hell!' The boys looked perturbed.

'I don't think I can come,' said Lee. I gotta help in my family's restaurant this evening. Then I have to stay in and do my homework.' The others looked at him in disgust.

'But I'll try and get out of it!' he added. 'I'll slip out if I can.'

'Sounds like a plan!' confirmed Gavin grimly.

'It is fun remember, Gav?' coaxed Reubin, his eyes widening and face now bursting with excitement. 'Maad!' he uttered for effect. Drew was desperate to spill the beans.

'I declare this meeting over!' proclaimed Gavin. 'Oh! In these bags are branded club pens and notebooks everyone. You need to be takin' notes of developments over the next weeks,' ended Gavin mysteriously.

'I bought in the latest copy of *Riff n' Roll*,' Raj said urgently.

'Next time Raj. Me and Drew gotta go quick.'

'It's got a double spread of Monster Metallions in it! They got a new album coming out, and they are gonna be touring!' Gavin and Drew stopped in their tracks, looking as if they'd been hit by a ten-ton truck.

'Nice one Raj!' cheered Drew finally. 'We'll look into it later!' and with that, the boys raced each other down the path, pushing each other out of the way as they went. Terry had a head start on them, so he got his own back by running streaks ahead of them across the little park.

Back on the main road they went their separate ways. 'Knock mi!' yelled Reubin to Gavin. *That was odd*, Raj thought to himself. Normally, Drew and Gavin would be fighting to see that magazine. *It must be something important, this friend of theirs*, he decided.

It was almost five o' clock. Once they were back home, Gavin and Drew raced up to see Zarok. He had made himself comfortable behind the boxes piled up in front of Gavin's bed.

There was a sheet hung up at the side of it that Zarok used like a curtain, but he was rather bored and just staring at the tree. He had caught up on some much-needed sleep, though he knew that he wouldn't need to do that every day. He was relieved to see the boys burst into their room to see him.

'Hiya!' he called out, jumping up at once.

'Hi Zarok! You been OK? Look Zarok! We wanna show you around before the parents get back. Do you wanna have a bath?'

'I don't know what a bath is!' Zarok shook his head sadly.

'A shower then!' Drew showed him the bathroom and how to work the shower. Then he took him downstairs on a tour of the house, before going to the back door in the kitchen.

'Kitchen's below our room, and just out here there is a kind of outside loo stuck on to it. It's mainly too cold to use, so it's a good hiding place! On the other side of it– see that? It's a tiny larder, the size of a phone box. Can you see on those shelves? There are loads of pears we picked. You can help yourself!' said Drew generously, pushing one into Zarok's hand.

'Just don't take too much fruit or veg in one go, in case they become suspicious,' warned Gavin. Next, Zarok went off to try the shower, while Drew and Gavin decided they would search for evidence that might lead to Zarok in the garden.

They started by cordoning it off, marking out a large area up to the back with garden canes. Drew came back with some tape.

'Not seltape, you idiot!' snarled Gavin.

'Shall I get masking tape then? Look! Do you think the police start messing around deciding what tape to use when they cordon off an area?!'

'Just put the tape on then, and I'll get some torches. It's getting dark.' Soon there were three torches shining upon their pitch and they took to their hands and knees scouring the area.

'I found something!' shouted Drew. It was an odd, small silver gadget.

'Put it in your pocket. I think we need spades, bruv.' Spades procured, the boys set to work enthusiastically (and needlessly digging), until there were potholes everywhere. Time was all but forgotten as they dug up more and more, before they found a rake to utilise. It would have been better if they had started with the rake. Suddenly, they were aware of Zarok's face at their window, waving at them. And the faces of others directly below, who didn't look quite so happy to see them at work. *Drat! The parents were back.* Gavin swung round wildly, his spade mid air.

'What on earth do you think you are doing?!' asked his mother. 'Gavin, Drew! What is the meaning of this?!'

Miriam Mason looked genuinely upset, shaking her head in disbelief. Their dad looked furious.

'Jaaaaaaas! What's with all the torches and canes, and you've made an absolute mess of my lawn! Isn't it enough that you've already dug up your mother's potatoes and bulbs she had planted for the spring?! It's just not on! Wise your bap! Put this spade back in the shed immediately and get inside!' finished their dad tersely, marching inside with his hand steadying their mother's shoulder. The boy's packed up and got inside. Their dad stood squarely in the middle of the kitchen.

'Twice in one week, practically. Just what are you playing at?!'

'We was just trying to help out dad,' said Drew with a soulful sigh.

'Help?! Guff!'

'We saw that there were lots of leaves and we took a rake to them, but the rake got stuck and, anyway, you are supposed to turn the soil over to let the air get to it,' finished Gavin with a flash of inspiration.

'Really! Well, since you must be weary after all your 'helpful' exertions; I expect you'll be needing an early night! You can turn in by 8.30!' And with a snort, their dad turned on his heels and trudged off, muttering to his wife, 'I'm off to watch the news.'

At least their parents had not seen Zarok, who had thrown himself back under Gavin's bed. But soon a howl was to be heard from the bathroom.

'What on earth!' cried their mum for the second time.

'What is it love?' called out their dad.

'There is a flood in the bathroom!' The parents stood in the bathroom observing the damage. It was not long-term damage, but the walls had evidently been given a soaking and the shower had been left on slightly, pumping water onto the floor, which was now seeping into the hall carpet. Soap was wedged in the plughole, water was cascading over the base of the shower and one of the taps was on full blast...

'Yikes,' uttered Drew. 'I'm really sorry mum. I'd forgotten I was going to have a shower. I got distracted. Billie must have...'

'No. Billie was with me!' retorted his mother firmly. 'It's not like you, Drew!' She crossed her eyebrows. Maybe the boys were tired and hungry and overworked at school,' she surmised. *After all... she and Brian worked long hours now.*

'Mudder mange! There's no hope for them to be sure!' deduced their father grimly as he returned to watch the news downstairs. Gavin and Drew fled to confront Zarok.

'Zarok, you can't do that in the shower. Me mum went ballistic!'

'I'm so sorry Drew. I tried to get your attention at your window. I couldn't get the pressure right, the shower is too good. Then I panicked and had to leave it when I heard your parents come back!'

'It's alright Zarok. It's not your fault. It's the shower's,' soothed Gavin.

Luckily, there was sweet potato on the menu for dinner and Drew and Gavin swiped them off their plates to give to Zarok. Then they took seconds and pocketed those for him. Fortunately, Miriam had made rice and peas and a stew (a dish shown to her by Honour), so there was plenty of nourishing food, which meant the boys could do without the extras. Zarok was ravenous and gratefully tucked into it.

'I wish I could thank your mother personally,' said Zarok sorrowfully. 'It is delicious!'

'Heck, imagine thanking her now?!' replied Drew. He had wanted to show Zarok the garden shed and give him a spare key. Perhaps it was a good thing that they had been summoned to take an 'early night' because it wouldn't seem odd that they weren't down in the front room watching TV! The boys explained this to Zarok, along with the day's events.

'That's great! I'm looking forward to seeing your buddies!' he replied.

Gavin scrutinised his new friend's features; the huge opaque eyes and the velvety, translucent, white skin that gave the appearance of being lit from the inside. When he smiled, you could not see his teeth as they were built into his gums. Only a small ridge at the edge of his gums betrayed that he had teeth. Gavin and Drew had got used to him by now, but what would their friends say or do?

Drew and Gavin didn't need to wait long to find out. A stone cracked against their window pane, and Drew looked out to see that Greg, Reubin and Raj were outside in their back garden, having taken the little path down the side of the house. Gavin flew down the rickety, wooden back stairs to let them in though the kitchen back door. The 'club members' had been wise to turn up together, so as to reduce the odds of them getting caught. But it was extra iffy now.

Zarok thought it would be better to get under the bed until the time was right for Gavin to introduce him. He was more nervous than the brothers and his little heart was beating even faster than usual. What if the boys that were coming were hostile to him and had alerted the police or told their parents? He knew his secrecy and his safety would then be compromised, and his picture would be in the papers and all over town. Zarok curled into a ball and hid his face, pulling his hoodie as tight as possible over him. Gavin was one for more circuitous proceedings, while Drew wasn't.

'When's your doops comin' then? I thought he was staying with you?' asked Greg, eyeing the boy's bedroom door hopefully. They had all sidled quietly up the back stairs and were safely in the boys' room, squeezed onto Drew's bed. Gavin sat beside his bed protectively. It was nice and cosy in the room, although it was big. Gavin realised it was a much better idea to have them all round than take Zarok to the allotment. Suddenly, Gavin put a finger to his lips and went: 'Shhh… Listen up Dogs of Hell! Our new friend will be nervous to meet you, and he's a special person… Er…He comes from a long way away, and he's not much like us. He might not be very well coz he's got an extra finger, and he doesn't want anyone to know he's staying, especially my parents, so…'

Gavin puckered his lips. This was tricky. He was waffling. Greg was wondering if this kid was an exchange student. But they weren't on a French exchange…

'I had a French exchange student once and he was bare weird too!' sympathised Greg.

'C'mon, just tell 'em Gav!' urged Reubin, who was dying to see Zarok and looked like he was about to burst a blood vessel. 'Crawb up, innit?!' (Which means something was looking good.) He started towards the sheet, and Gavin shoved him off. 'Crawb off!'

'Our new friend's name is Zarok… And you know, he comes from America… Well, he doesn't come from there exactly because he's a Black Eyed Kid and when you see him you gotta shut up, and keep quiet coz…' But Drew couldn't stand this prevaricating any longer!

'WE GOT *AN ALIEN,* HELL DOGS!!' Right on cue, Zarok peeped out from behind the sheet wearing his most engaging smile, and holding out his palms in a gesture of appeasement.

'O-M-GEE!!' shouted Raj. 'Holy Moley-Holy Moley-Holy-Moley!!! *IT'S A FREAKIN' ALIEN!* AAAARRGHH!!!' as he shot up to hop from foot to foot, unable to contain himself. *How could he help but wail?! And be taken by surprise!*

'*Whoa…TURN I' UP!'* WOW! WOWZER!!!' Reubin burst out simultaneously with Raj at the thunderbolt revelation. 'You pulled it out the bag this time, Gav…He's freakin' *dope,* bruv!!' he breathed, awestruck and starry-eyed.

'Yes! I did pull it out the bag, didn't I, Reubin?!' piped up Drew at once. He was miffed. *After all, who had seen him first…*

Astounded, Reubin and Greg stared long and hard at the brothers' find in amazement…

'*Do yu ting…*' mumbled Reubin with a quizzical look at Zarok, taking in his alien form.

'MAAAD!' Greg, finally exclaimed at (a grinning Drew). Hands on his head, he looked dumbfounded as for once something really was mad! The boy's eyes looked as though they would literally pop out of their sockets! Drew hugged himself with delight.

'Throwing himself towards Zarok to embrace him, Reubin vigorously shook his hand up and down, chuckling like crazy. Gavin and Drew were swollen with pride. (Being quiet was all but forgotten, as this was the reaction they had really hoped for.)

'MAAAD!' whooped Reubin along with Greg now. *As if he could keep quiet*?! He hadn't doubted Gavin, but seeing was believing…Remembering that he was supposed to 'shut-up' (and catching himself), he started to roll around the floor instead, creased up with suppressed hysterics before hurling himself around the room like a dervish, trying to contain himself. Finally, he jumped up issuing a joyful 'Brrrap!' The fervent others joined in, laughing happily and trying to roll their r's better than each other. The brother's room quickly became a 'Brapping' riot!

When Gavin shouted, 'Someone shut Raj up!' (as he was still 'Holy Moly-ing…') Greg tackled the shaking, shrieking boy, pushed him face down on the bed, and started to pummel him with a pillow, so that his muffled Holy-Moleys were now stifled. *It seemed that ecstatic yelps were admitted but petrified ones weren't!*

'S'Reubin too!' sobbed Raj between breaths. Zarok's eyes were now shining as he marvelled at his new-found friends.

'Zarok? Is that your name? Are you really an alien, mate?!' enthused Greg at last. 'Cool! That is *sooo cool!* RAD! *How cool is that?!*' Greg's reaction differed to Raj's in that – despite being overcome – he tried desperately to stay unflustered.

'Braap?' smiled Zarok offering his thumb. Meanwhile, another succession of 'OMGs' from Raj were suppressed under the bed covers. Reubin winced.

'Breathe easy, Raj bruv!' said Reubin kindly, realising he was in (serious) shock.

When the commotion died down, the boys sat in a circle in front of the alien wearing a combo of ecstatic and shocked expressions. This lot had never been as lost for words as they were now. Raj had now calmed down a bit, but with his eyes like saucers, he still looked startled.

'This is gonna be a blast, innit?! I wish Lee was here,' said Greg, who wanted to get to grips with it all. 'Lee needs to be here! He will probably know about your kind of spacemen… knowing him!' He squeezed his chin, lost in thought.

'Yeah!' agreed Reubin, looking thoughtful.

'C'n you beatbox thingy?' asked Greg inquisitively.

'Sure!' volunteered Zarok obligingly.

'He can't' mouthed Reubin from across the room at him (his eyebrows raised).

'Don't worry. Me n' Gavin and Reubin n' Raj will teach ya beatboxing! Not Drew though, coz he's rubbish. He just blows raspberries…' Drew jumped up.

'I can beatbox very well, thank you very much!' replied Drew, hot with indignation. 'I c'n beatbox to Rap-hed Rong'n's Get it from da get get ghetto!'

'Alright doops! Do you wanna stay here or go home?' enquired Greg of Zarok bluntly.

'I would like to get back home, but it will be difficult,' answered the alien shyly.

'We'll help you!' shouted Reubin. 'We'll all help you, won't we Greg!'

'One more time!' agreed Greg.

'He's going to stay with us first!' cut in Gavin indignantly. 'How dy'a think you're going to help him get home anyway, clever clogs?!' Reubin was a bit stumped.

'Mind you, you know America coz you're from there, aren't you?' said Drew.

'Yes, but I ain't never been there! You going to be in our club, The Dogs of Hell, Zarok?!' asked Reubin, cheerfully unabashed.

'He's from the Devil's Highway!' boasted Drew. 'He's what's called a Black Eyes Kid, aren't you Zarok!'

'Eyed!' corrected Gavin.

'Do ya mind if you move your hoodie a bit so I can see you better?' asked Greg. 'Cool!'

'Zarok tentatively let his hoodie fall away, whereupon Raj let out a blood-curdling scream.

'You prat Raj! You eejit!' shouted Reubin.

'It's OK, it's OK,' mollified Drew. It was not OK! Footsteps tramped down the hall, and the bedroom door was flung open! Zarok, with lightning speed, threw himself back under the bed.

'Right enough is enough!' Miriam said, casting her eye around at the sea of boys.

'You Greg and Raj! You should be at home. You can come round at normal hours, so I don't know what is the need for these high jinx! And Reubin, I'm going to have to tell your mother about this. It's Gavin and Drew's fault, of course!' All the time, Greg's hand was clamped over Raj's mouth.

'I'm so sorry if I was rude to him… I didn't know…' stammered Raj distressed.

'What?!' questioned Drew and Gavin's irate mother.

'It's nine o' clock! Everybody out! All of you get home straightaway and I'll talk to you two in the morning!' asserted Miriam, turning a steely eye on her boys. The friends all tramped down the stairs together and took off into the late evening. *That was a close call*, they realised.

'I knew Raj would freak out!' said Gavin, looking fed up.

'He won't tell anyone though,' Drew replied, defending his friend.

'I liked all of your friends Drew and Gavin,' affirmed Zarok. 'I am so happy, much happier than I have been in a long time! And this gadget you found for me is a transmitter. It's mine. Thank you for finding it. I cannot use it in England though…'

'I know it was a bit iffy Zarok. But there's strength in numbers. With all our mates together, we will help you! We will find a way to get you back home if that is what you really want… I don't want you to go like, but the Dog's of Hell can do anything whatsoever…easily, if we can find a way…'

'Almost anything Gav!' spluttered Drew in dismay. But he had an inkling that they might have bitten off more than they could chew this time.

CHAPTER FOUR

A NEW RECRUIT JOINS THE CLUB

Zarok amused himself while the boys were at school by doing some drawing. He had found some paper, coloured pencils and felt-tips and began a set of pictures of his new-found friends. They were bold and zany and the likenesses were very good. He took the step of dressing them in the kind of spacesuits that he knew of back home on his own planet. As he busied himself with the detail, he saw that he had captured the personalities of each of the boys. As Terry had been missing, he drew him without a face.

It was pleasant down time for him and he kept his energy levels up with a bowl of sweet potatoes and a glass of water beside him. With no one home he could dress down in a T-shirt and shorts. He felt contented, and above all, safe. After a time engaged in this activity, he stopped to take out a bottle of castor oil the boys had given him. Slathering it over his skin, he felt much better as it did his delicate skin good.

Feeling a little adventurous, he opted to walk out and about in the upstairs hall. There was a large window near the top of the stairs and on the window ledge was a number of cacti on display. Zarok's eyes lit up. He picked up a prickly cactus and took a bite out of it. He had planned to take just one bite but found it so tasty, he munched the whole thing, spikes and all. After his drawings were finished, he felt like braving the house and garden. There was someone at home however, and Roji the dog started barking like mad, picking up Zarok's scent.

Back in the playground at Higglesdon Wick Juniors, Terry was on Drew's case.

'I know you lot are keeping something from me! Bet everyone was round yours last night, and I bet it wasn't exactly your Auntie Faggot that's come to stay!' Terry looked hurt. 'I *can* keep a secret Drew…Go on! Tell us!' This was hard for Drew.

'It's case sensitive…We were testing the waters first!'

'Don't talk to me in club language! If you don't tell us, maybe I'll find out anyway, and then I won't keep it a secret!'

'That's blackmail Terry! I tell ya, I'll ask my brother and I bet you can know about it tomorrow!' vouched Drew, slinging his bag over his back.

'You know I want ya to know Tezza, but it could be that Gav don't like you hanging out with Sergio, you know he ain't in the club,' added Drew craftily.

'He lives next door to me an' he plays footie. And I bet I'll find out about it before tomorrow!' Terry called after him.

As soon as school was out, Drew and Gavin tore home as fast as their legs could carry them. The arrangement was that they would hold the club meeting in their roomy garden shed. Greg, Reubin, Raj and Lee would turn up ten minutes after them. As soon as they got in, the boys raced upstairs to get Zarok and escort him to the shed. It would be his first meeting of the Dogs of Hell. But when they got to their room, Zarok was gone! There was a moment of panic in Gavin's searching green eyes.

'Oh no! Where's he got to! Zaaarok?!' he yelled. Drew dashed downstairs, giving the house the once over and looking under every sofa. Gavin went straight down to the shed, only to find Zarok sitting, propped up on the lawnmower. Drew soon caught up.

'Phew! Thanks for that Zarok!' gasped Drew.

The garden shed had a thick wooden surface that went nearly all the way down one side. There were a couple of fixed vices on there, and all kinds of bits and bobs in boxes and jars, from nails to screws and washers. It was stocked with tools a plenty. All sorts of stuff resided at the back, including rusty bikes and wheels, spades and rakes and a huge deflated dinghy. It was packed to the rafters, yet still there was space in the middle for a bench, stripy deckchairs, plus a couple of stools. But as they took in the familiar space, there were differences to be observed.

It was evident that Zarok had been busy that afternoon. The tools, including various saws, had been nailed to the wooden walls in a neat, convenient arrangement that made them easy to find and use. It also showed them off to good effect. The hammers and chisels and screwdrivers had all been sorted out properly and given an organised place. A couple of new shelves had appeared, and all the jars stood in a row on them. The workspace was now free of the mountains of curly wood shavings on the surface and floor, but that was not all. Rubbish had been put into bin bags and the back area was tidy and spacious. A square of material had been put up against the window. This would be useful when Zarok went undercover there, but also made it look homely. Now that the electric light was on, it looked like an inviting space to either work or hang out in.

'Wow! Good job Zarok!' exclaimed Drew, impressed.

'This is really cool in here, but it's still got that nice smell of wood. No sawdust everywhere though!' approved Gavin, as he walked the length of it and perched on his bike, which had been polished up and allocated space to move. Zarok gazed at them, smiling contentedly.

'It was nothing, it gave me something to do! I hope you like the shelf. It will hold out nice and strong!'

'Bang! Bang! Bang!' The Dogs of Hell were at the door clamouring to come in. This time, Lee was with them. He had been told about Zarok and was bracing himself. He was, however, quite a passive boy. The shed door opened and the boys fell in.

'Hullo Zarok! Safe!' greeted Reubin, slapping him on the back.

'How yer doing Zarok dups!' hailed Greg, beaming madly at their alien find. At the same time, he was stopping himself from running!

'Hiya Zarok!? Pleased to meet you!' said Lee, smiling gently as he extended a hand, not wanting to alarm the alien. He was shaking a little.

'Notice how none of you lot are saying hello to us!' scolded a miffed Drew.

'Like it's only our shed and our club!'

'It's his shed now by the looks of it,' offered up Greg cheerfully.

'Nice one, Zarok!' Raj was on his best behaviour today and felt a bit ashamed of making such a scene the night before.

'Good to see you, Zarok. I'm sorry I was so rude to you last night…'

'Yeah and the rest, blah, blah, blah…' cut in Reubin bluntly.

'That's OK Raj dude. I understand why you would be freaked out by me! I don't suppose you have met a Black Eyed Kid before.'

'Alright, order! I declare this meeting open!' shouted Gavin with gusto, grabbing a hammer and bashing it on the surface for effect. The others had all found a place to sit and styled their ties around their heads.

'This is a special occasion for us!' began Gavin, who was the only one standing.

'As you can see, we will soon initiate a new member into our club! It is of course, Zarok! Never, ever on Earth, since time began, has an alien from outer space joined forces with a band of earthlings! But here today, you lot, not only are we here to welcome a Black Eyed Kid by the name of Zarok, but never in the history of mankind has a club called The Dogs of Hell admitted a...'

There was a sharp rap on the door, followed by an equally sharp rap at the window. It sounded impatient!

'Crikey...' went Reubin, pulling a face at Drew. *Shell dun!*

'Excuse me, Mason family!' came an old lady's shrilly tone. Will you do me the kindness of lending me a spanner? Sorry to disturb!' Gavin grabbed a spanner while Reubin turned off the light.

'It's only 'ole Mrs Small from next door,' he said, moving towards the door to unlock it.

'She can't see very well,' hissed Drew to Zarok. The door then burst open and in waded Terry sporting a flowery headscarf!

'Thanks for inviting me to the meeting comrades!' he yelled cheerily, taking a little curtsy in front of the seated boys.

'Secrets out!' stated Reubin in a monotone voice. Zarok's hood was pulled right over as he looked down at his knees.

Now Greg couldn't help himself. It had been bad enough as it was, keeping this from Terry.

'Drew n' Gav's guest's a 'Black Eyed Kid', aren't you Zarok!'

'Wh-aat?!' No way! You *are* kidding me! Don't do jokes like that, man!' asserted Terry, his awestruck eyes firmly on the club's new recruit to be.

'You afraid of him, Terry?' cajoled Raj, as if he hadn't been himself!

'You're a fine one to talk,' sniped Gavin, gaping at his friend.

'No! I'm not afraid. I don't bleev you!' quested Terry, going a little pale.

'Not all this again!' said Drew resolutely. 'Let's get on with it! Our visitor here is called Zarok and he's a Black Eyed Kid all the way from America, aren't you Zarok?' There was an awkward silence. Terry laughed a nervously. This wasn't like the Terry who was usually robust and a bit of a joker.

'Let me see him then!' said Terry finally, going deathly white.

'We've all sworn to secrecy Terry and you've got to as well! Otherwise, there's gonna be big trouble for all of us, especially Zarok!' This was awkward. It was clear that Terry did not see this altogether as fun.

'Excuse me bruv…' Terry said to the hooded figure before addressing the others.

'Yikes!' he mouthed to the others, rolling his eyes.

'It's just that I have heard about Black Eyed Kids! I read about it somewhere and they're dangerous man! He could kill us!' Raj began to sob uncontrollably, clapping his hand over his mouth.

'Did 'e ask to use your fone?!' went on Terry in an audible whisper.

Then Zarok spoke. What a relief, as you could have cut the tension with a knife. *They must have been right to try and keep it from Terry. He might betray them all now!*

'Terry is right everyone. I have tried to tell you that Black Eyed Kids have a terrible reputation. They terrorise everyone on the Devil's Highway, and that's why they didn't like me. I'm not like them, Dudes! I think you can tell by now that I mean no harm,' Zarok said, shrinking back.

'What are you doing here, then?' retorted Terry acidly.

'He wants to get back home! Now sit down and shut up!' instructed Drew. Terry hesitated before sitting himself down quietly and patting Drew as he did so.

'Before we had to put up with an intrusion from a club member, who might soon be an ex-club member at this rate...' began Gavin majestically, 'we were going to welcome a new member into the Dogs of Hell! Will you swear an oath of allegiance to the club, Zarok?' (*'Yes, I swear an oath of allegiance to the club'*) hissed Drew to Zarok. Zarok repeated the words in his American drawl.

'Do you abide by the Dogs of Hell's rules?' continued Gavin sternly.

'I abide by the Dogs of Hell's rules!' echoed Zarok heartily.

'Then, I welcome you, we all welcome you, as a fully-fledged member!'

'Every hell dog has his day!' shouted the assembled members (which was a routine mantra.)

At last, the mood was lightened and the boys all cheered, slapping Zarok on the back. He stood up and formally shook all their hands before joining in with a zealous salute, and the deal was done.

'We have other important initiation rites,' added Gavin importantly, 'but we won't do 'em today, except you can sign this book in red.' Dutifully Zarok signed it. Terry's eyes affixed on Zarok the whole way through the proceedings with a look of astonishment on his face. Suddenly, Terry laughed, seeming to relax into the idea, he finally said: 'This is going to be one hell of a ride!' All the time he had been flicking bits of sodden toilet paper at the walls, which landed with a satisfying splat. Zarok observed him with interest, hoping that he could trust him.

There was another knock on the shed door. This time it was Billie.

'Are you coming in Drew? It's my dolly's birthday today!'

'No flippin' way!' replied Drew. 'Hey Billie, you got any cake for her birthday? Bring it out to us and get us some Coca-Cola!'

'Alright Drew. It's chocolate cake!'

'Hurry up then!' Soon the cake arrived, and the door firmly shut on Billie who looked crestfallen. Meanwhile, Zarok had produced his drawings of the boys and pencilled in Terry's face on the remaining one. They were put up on display for them all to admire.

'Mine's the coolest!' enthused Reubin.

'We will talk properly later,' whispered Lee to Zarok. 'I'd like to find out more about you. You are not just a novelty and we must find a way to help you.'

'Thank you Lee. I'd like that,' replied Zarok, reassured.

'Changing the subject,' interjected Raj, producing his copy of *Riff n' Roll* again, 'When are we gonna check this out?'

'I've already been saving for when the Monster Metallions come to town coz they come every year!' said Gavin, who not only did a paper round, but had also saved his pocket money, and had been paid for chores.

'They play at Donnington and we are not old enough to go!' complained Greg.

'As if they're going to play Higglesdon Wick!'

'They might play at Readsford!'

'I'm going somehow mate, and what's more I'm gonna try and take Zarok too!' The Dogs of Hell discussed the implications of this.

'Listen up! One of their new releases has the words, 'Black Eyed Kid' in it!' revealed Raj excitedly.

'Gaan! Coincidence or what?!' They all poured over the lyrics. This added to Zarok's importance even more.

'Anything else!' shouted Gavin. 'You all gotta go in a minute!'

The cake had been expertly sliced so that everyone got an exact amount, yet they were still squabbling over it.

'Yeah! I saw your dad go into the bookies again today!' smiled Terry, waiting for a reaction.

'Go on!' pressed Drew, going a bit red.

'He looked as if he couldn't get in there fast enough. He was with a bloke. They looked glum when they came out!'

'Alright, don't milk it!' But Drew was worried. He would soon have to tell the others that his dad had a serious gambling problem because he needed their help! Terry reached down to procure another slither of wet toilet roll, fashioned it into a wodge and flung it at the wall with a resounding splat.

'Hey, don't Tez, Zarok just cleaned it up in here!'

'Why did he leave loads of wet bog roll around then?' protested Terry. A couple of other members of the Dogs of Hell had joined in the activity absently, so that a constellation of white splodges now decorated the walls.

On the whole, the meeting had been a success. Zarok had been accepted, and Terry seemed to have been won over. He had probably made a stink as he'd been sore about being left out at first. It was decided that Zarok would make himself at home in the shed that night. When all the boys had gone home, Zarok said: 'Gavin… I think I need to stretch my legs tonight, and I'd like to go out. Of course, I'll wear my hoodie in such a way that I am concealed. If you can find me a little of your sister's bronzer powder, it would be better.'

'What's that?'

'He means foundation. It's crap girls wear on their face. I'll get some for you, Zarok. Where are you going?' asked Drew.

'Just out and about for a couple of hours; when the streets are quiet.'

'Just be quiet when you go and come back!'

'Yes. Thank you, Drew! Do you mind finding me a sleeping bag? I'd like to get some sleep now, and you and Gavin must find time for your homework and family this evening!'

Zarok was right, of course, as it might start to look suspicious. Such a prospect didn't fill the boys with any enthusiasm at all. They wanted to be with Zarok, and check up on him all the time. This was still massive to them.

'*I mean an alien?!*' the boys kept saying to each other. The next day passed rather uneventfully. The boy's parents seemingly suspected nothing, and so Zarok lived quietly with the Masons as an invisible guest. There was just one thing that caused Gavin and Drew to sweat. In the middle of the night, the church bells rang out. A raucous chorus of clanging was not the norm at that time. It was likely to have woken up the whole neighbourhood! Drew and Gavin had feared the worst; it coincided with the time that Zarok had planned to go out! But the boys had fallen asleep and promptly forgotten about it, maybe preferring to forget…

The next evening, Drew approached his dad, who was sat in front of the fire reading the newspaper. He'd remembered there was what the boys called a 'madhouse' down the road, and he'd heard a neighbour say that it helped people with compulsive behaviour. Drew recalled that Mr Jackson had described gambling as compulsive behaviour.

'You feelin' alright this evening, dad?' asked Drew brightly, entering the front room with a leaflet behind his back. His father ignored him and looking for rugby scores, turned to the sports pages.

'Have you had a nice day, dad?' tried Drew again.

'Yes Drew,' replied his dad uncommittedly.

'Oh that's good, that's really good dad!' continued Drew. His dad scrunched the paper noisily and banged it down on his lap.

'And it would be even nicer if I could get five minutes peace!' he declared.

Drew remained there, wearing a rather fake looking smile.

'Oh! What's this? Look here... Something seems to have fallen out of the paper, dad. Some kind of leaflet. Here dad, it might be important!' announced Drew kindly, before slapping it on the side of the armchair. His father gave Drew a menacing look, before returning to his paper, so that his face was obscured inside it. Drew then sat in the front room, homework on his knee, waiting to see if his dad would take up the leaflet.

'Homework?' asked his dad in a monotone voice.

'I got it here on my knee, dad.' He might as well wait and see this through...

Soon, his mum came in with a couple of shirts and set one on the ironing board, switching the iron on. She decided to do a few dresses too and went out again, returning with them.

Then, Brian proceeded to tell her about the sports news and his mother listened with apparent interest, giving appropriate replies. In fact, she appeared to like hearing about the local football team.

'Any other local news, Brian?'

'Yes, though nothing spectacular. It seems that shops staying open late night are causing a few problems. There's a couple of space-fillers. Do you remember that awful churchbell racket in the middle of the night?!'

'Yes, indeed. How odd! Quare it was to be sure...'

'Well, obviously some prankster had got into the bell tower. The church warden said that it was not scheduled and he's looking for clues pointing to an intruder.'

'Aye! Good thing too!' said Miriam.

'And I don't know if this is related, same page... Some kid ambled into the late night store, you know, Paymoores, and asked if he could have a blueberry sodapop. Shopkeeper says, 'Of course, sonny,' then the kid walked off with six of them without paying... Apparently, it left the shopkeeper with a funny feeling, as if the boy truly didn't know you had to pay, and he shut up shop! He has no memory of the kid's face... Sounds like a muppet, if you ask me.'

'Drew was knitting his brow together into a wretched knot whilst gritting his teeth. *Yikes! It was obviously Zarok– he just knew it! Can't leave the room to find Zarok n' Gav. It would be too obvious...*

'How odd! Tis quare,' said Miriam again. 'At least our children aren't like that.'

'I dunno though...' muttered Brian, looking at Drew dubiously. After a few minutes, Drew decided to get more food, asking: 'Can I have seconds, mum?'

'Yes, but don't spill it everywhere.' Drew ran to find Gavin, who was playing games with Reubin upstairs. Zarok was watching, partially hidden under the bed's lower curtain.

Drew quickly relayed the information he'd just heard to Gavin.

'We best get you out of here and into the shed tonight, Zarok. Just for your own safety. That news has weirded us out!'

'You jus' can't do that, Zarok! You have to pay for fizzy drink or pop, whatever you call it… and the church bells… Cripes!'

'I'd forgotten that!' added Gavin.

'Why did you get up to the bell tower? I thought you were supposed to be good! That's what vampires do!'

'I said I am not bad; that I'm not evil, Drew! I didn't say that I could be good all the time. I can be naughty too, like you.' Poor Zarok looked ashamed, his eyes boring into the purple flowery duvet until the patterns blurred. Reubin pulled his hat round purposefully, and stood over Zarok.

'You can't do that, Zarok. Simples! That's the last time, *zeen*? Next time they'll call the po po and then it will be…' Reubin did a motion of slicing a finger through his neck. 'Think of 'ole Gavin and Drew trying to do their best to hide you blud yana?! *Likkle more…*'

And that was the end of that. Soon afterwards, Reubin left and Drew and Gavin went to bed feeling most perturbed. Downstairs, the leaflet that Drew had left for his dad had barely been glanced at. It was crumpled up instead and thrown in the bin.

Brian turned to Miriam and said, 'I took a bit o' time out with Geoff. We took a bite to eat at a new sandwich bar. It was very good I might add. Then, we nipped into the bookies to collect the winnings on his bet. Turns out there were great odds on the bet I lodged for him. Well, not that great odds, which is why he won handsomely! I tell you he was very grateful to me.'

'How much did he win?'

'He won about £80!' I'd have a flutter myself if I thought I could be as lucky. Some chance!'

CHAPTER FIVE
SPLODS

The next day was the start of the weekend. On Saturday morning, Brian or Miriam would make a cooked breakfast for all the family. It was usually a very pleasant atmosphere as they sat down and ate it together around the kitchen table. Gavin arrived in the kitchen earliest, having completed his paper round in record time. He'd got better and quicker at it, and now took Roji along with him to scare the other dogs (that scared him) as he posted his papers through the letterboxes.

'I'm glad you took the dog with you. He's unsettling me rather,' Miriam said to Gavin as she handed Brian a dozen eggs. Gavin gulped inwardly, knowing full well that the dog had been having barking fits and was prone to prowling around growling since Zarok had moved in. Gavin suddenly felt guilty on account of his parents.

Should he tell them the truth?

'Mummm,' began Gavin slowly. 'You know that...?'

'Yes Gavin?' prompted his mum, hands on hips, waiting.

'You know that Frayre's coming today? What time's she coming?'

'I'm not sure. Are you sure that's what you want to tell me?'

Gavin hesitated and hurriedly thought the better of it. Anyway, it would be better to discuss it with Drew first, and wait until his parents were in a good mood. There was a bit of an atmosphere.

'I think Roji's not well. He must have worms as he's barking a lot!'

'I doubt it!' replied Brian blandly, as he grilled the bacon rashers to perfection. Drew then sloped in still wearing his pyjamas, his eyes crusty with sleep.

'Morning!' he said to noone in particular.

'Can you set the plates up and go and wake Billie again?' asked his mum.

'What? Both at the same time? What do you think I am, bionic?' protested Drew, putting his plate down and taking two steps out of the room to shout for Billie. Soon, Alex (who had arrived in silence and taken his usual seat) and Billie were sat around the table with Drew, Gavin and Miriam and Brian.

'Well, this looks delicious, though I say it myself!' exclaimed Brian heartily.

'Tuck in everyone!' There were a couple of sausages each, bacon and eggs, beans for the children and tomato for the grown-ups, plus some yummy mushrooms accompanied by crispy fried bread.

'Not a bad little starter!' declared Drew enthusiastically as he wolfed down mouthful after mouthful. Some general banter went down, before Miriam broke off.

'Hmmm! I don't want to create any controversy but… While I remember, there are 'splobs' appearing everywhere– on the newly plastered dining room wall, in the hall, bathroom…and…' She trailed off looking puzzled.

'Splobs?' repeated Brian, his mouth full of juicy tomato. Miriam was genuinely puzzled over the appearance of the splobs and how they had got there, and how more kept appearing, as if they were a self-multiplying phenomenon.

'Er… What do splobs look like mum?' asked Gavin innocently.

'If anyone knows, I'm sure you do!' put in Alex witheringly.

'Oh look, there's one over there!' exclaimed Miriam. Sure enough, splayed upon the nice red paint, was a so-called white 'splob' that stood out unmistakably.

'Cutting to the chase, how many are there?' asked Brian grimly.

'About seventeen and counting…' replied Miriam, still perplexed. Brian investigated the one before him.

'They are obviously dollops of wet toilet paper that have been lobbed at the wall and then stuck! Drew?' Drew assumed a look of astonishment, his mouth crammed with toast. It was, in fact, news to him.

'Well, at least it isn't something that's gone wrong with the plaster,' said Miriam, casting her mind back to the mystery appearances of the last few days.

'No, but it's disrespectful. Boys, you are not five year olds. I'm cut to the onions with all the drama round here. It's not good enough! You will sort them out today. They dry hard and might take the paintwork off with them, so be gentle!'

'I've seen them and I think they are nice, like stars!' said Billie.

'I didn't do it!' protested Drew. Gavin realised that it was better to admit one of them *had* done it, as he had a sinking feeling that it must be Zarok!

'Um I did it, sorry!' he said shortly, looking glum.

'I don't know!' went on his mum. 'It's one thing after another. Odd things like the dog acting strangely, bells ringing at night, and now I remember something else! Four kilos of sweet potatoes have been gone through, my big bottle of vinegar has disappeared and so has 1lb of molasses. I needed that for a cake!

My bottle of castor oil has gone missing too! Added to which, my cacti's either walked off or been crunched into!'

'Drew?' said Brian blandly.

'It's not me!' he replied indignantly. Gavin was starting to fear their secret was on its way out. He imagined it was time for some amateur dramatics to serve as cover.

'It's not fair!' he burst out. 'Me n' Drew don't get any attention. It's all Billie this and Billie that. You spend a fortune on them; like Frayre too with her rubbishy costumes, and what do me and Drew get? Nothing!' He pulled at his short hair for emphasis, conveying a look of utter disgust. He raged on…

'We dint get to the fireworks, and dad's got my fone for himself and I've not got it back!'

'OK! Let's not spoil this nice breakfast!' broke in Miriam hastily. The pleasant Saturday morning banter was turning into a blazing row.

'It's too late!' wailed Gavin. 'While Frayre and Billie get everything in the world, me and Drew won't even get to the concert. Well, I might, but I've had to spend a year doing paper rounds and chores!' Gavin had made himself red with fury. Drew was impressed.

'I wish I hadn't started this!' fussed Miriam, visibly upset. Brian looked annoyed and as a stone-cold look crept across his features, the boys feared it more than an angry outburst. But their dad now looked momentarily pacified. *Result?*

'I will concede, that it's not all bad. You boys have done a grand job sorting out my shed. The tools hanging up look splendid, and you really have organised it very well! I also noticed that you sorted out the light fitting across the work surface… So, I am impressed, and I had decided to give you back your things, plus arrange some extra pocket money, which I'm sure would be appreciated. But now you are making it hard for me. What's happened to mum's kitchen things?!'

'I dunno!' answered Drew without hesitation.

'I had to bring 'em in for science,' explained Gavin. 'We're making an organic clock and we need things for…for energy and stuff!'

'Stop acting the maggot! Couldn't you have asked your mother first? Are basic manners so hard to come by, or am I old fashioned and everyone just helps themselves to another's things nowadays?!'

'There wasn't time. Mum had left for work and I forgot!' replied Gavin, thinking on his feet and giving every explanation under the sun. His dad paused, staring into his empty plate.

'Alright! Let us stall the ball. Since you have done my shed so well, which I will not only be using today, but likely to utilise much more frequently, we will draw a line under it. I am going to reach out to you with a gesture of goodwill, which is to give you enough pocket money to cover your concert tickets, meaning that my good faith needs to translate to you, as an act that will make you, in turn, respect our household. No more swiping your mum's things and no more splobs!' he finished firmly. The family all parted their separate ways, while Gavin and Drew remained in the kitchen drinking second cups of tea and feeding Roji sausages.

'Reesult!' yelped Drew when his dad was firmly out of hearing.

'I dunno,' said Gavin. 'He's gonna be using the blasted shed more! It's worked against us. We can't hide Zarok in Frayre's now when she's back…'

'What about the tickets though?' said Drew, leaning into his brother conspiratorially. 'You can already buy one. So guess who the other two can be bought for!' Drew looked ready to burst with excitement.

'I know! It will be amazing to take Zarok to see the Monster Metallions!'

'It will be the best night EVER??!' The two boys leapt up and danced around the room before descending into a bout of headbanging. They couldn't wait to flee upstairs and tell Zarok the good news, totally forgetting that he had nearly brought big trouble on them over the splobs.

Frayre sailed in on a cloud of perfume with a huge magenta rucksack.

'Hi boys!' she greeted them, going over to hug both her brothers. 'Catch up soon!' she said, sailing out just as quickly, shouting, 'I'm going to find mum! MUM?!'

Then Alex came in and slapped some money on the table.

'Dad's given me this to give to you. Got out of that one nicely didn't you! If I were you I'd put your money in the bank before you screw it up, wet it and turn it into splobs!' he said as he strolled out waving a handful of notes at them, which was more than they had. But it was Alex's own money.

The two boys grabbed the money and ran out of the room, racing each other up the stairs whooping like anything. Throwing their door open wide they couldn't wait to fall upon Zarok and tell him the good news; that all three of them could afford to go to the concert! They flung the curtain aside. OMG! Just an empty bed awaited them. Zarok was not there!

'Aargh! He must be in the garden shed!' shouted Drew, going over to the window. Damn! His father was walking purposefully over to the garden shed with half a shelving unit.

'DAD!' shouted Drew out of the window, throwing up the sash as he did so.

'Don't shout, don't go in!' commanded Gavin fiercely. The boys had to think of something fast.

'Dad! Wait a minute, Geoff's at the door!' Brian stood in his tracks. *That was odd.* Geoff lived the other side of Higglesdon Wick and was really a work colleague. He hesitated. Then, he put his wood down by the shed door and strolled back towards the house. The boys were already halfway down the stairs, and within seconds, had burst into the shed. They grabbed Zarok by the scruff of his neck and hauled him towards the kitchen with a cloth over his head, and up the back stairs. All of their hearts were pumping wildly – Gavin felt as if he was about to have a heart attack. This was the closest shave ever!

How lucky was that?! As the boys stood over the banister, listening to what was happening in the front part of the house, it just so happened that someone *was* at the door. It was such a busy household, there was always someone calling for someone. Miriam was expecting Honour that morning, for example. But it was the postman this time with a hefty parcel for Brian, so their dad was very pleased not to have missed him. Miriam was in her box dressing room with Frayre and had not noticed the bell. *Good, the boys were trying to behave.*

Back in their bedroom, flinging themselves on to the bed, the boys whooped for joy over and over.

'Zarok! We can all go to the concert!'

The splobs were all but forgotten. 'You can't just shin down the drainpipe and off to the shed anymore as dad's going to use it more! He liked your handiwork a bit too much!'

'I should really like to see the Monster Metallions, Gavin and Drew. I hope it will be dark enough in there for me not to cause a stir!'

'Yeah, it'll be dark! That's the whole point. You'll never be recognised! Even on the train there it will be dark…in the evening…' Drew tapered off doubtfully.

'It'll be alright. Hoodie, sunglasses, job done!' said Gavin decisively.

'Sunglasses. Good call!' drawled the vacant looking alien smiling avidly, thereby revealing his toothless, stony gums.

Suddenly, there was a scream from the attic. Frantic footsteps followed and another holler was emitted in the hallway.

'Arrgh! Boys! WHAT have you done to my tanning booth?!' Next thing Frayre burst through the door as Zarok had dived under the covers.

'Come and have a look at what you've done!' she yelled, her frizzy new up-do making her look even wilder with fury. She stuck her head back out of their room and shrieked, 'Muuum! Come up to the attic and look what they've done!'

'Get out!' growled Drew rudely, wondering whether to face the music or make himself scarce. The brothers were soon mooching up the stairs. Frayre had an inflatable tanning booth arrangement that was set up with a neat trestle table containing all her lotions and potions. There was not too much of a mess, Drew observed.

'There is to me!' screamed Frayre. 'Just look at it! And you're not even allowed in here!' Gavin and Drew took in the black inflatable booth. It was speckled with fake tan, which had somehow strayed to the walls as well. Tissues, sodden with the tan, had been fashioned into dollops (no doubt lobbed), and her groovy cerise and lime wallpaper was splattered with 'splobs'.

'Oh, oh!' cried Gavin ironically.

'Boys!' exclaimed their mother hotly. 'Not again! More splobs?!'

Turning on her brothers angrily, Fraye shouted accusingly, 'Why the heck have you been trying out my spray tan kit, and why would you not even bother to hide the evidence?!'

'Do you know, my tanning booth is new?!'

'Alright! We haven't popped it or used it as a dinghy!' groaned Gavin.

'It's really naughty boys! Really! To use it and not even clean up? The nozzle on her spray is all clogged up, and the mess has dried…'

'To come in *my room* at all! Let alone mess about. They were probably mud wrestling knowing them!'

'That's a good idea!' said Drew airily.

'Good idea?' screeched Frayre, now brandishing her spray tan and blasting it at Drew's face. Luckily, it hit his chin.

'Now don't do that Frayre. It's dangerous! Say sorry Gavin!'

'Who said it was me? It was him! It was Billie!'

'I very much doubt it! Gavin! Help your sister make her booth good again. It's not nice for her to come home and find her stuff used!'

'*Used!* It's been made an utter mess of and wasted!' hollered Frayre, glaring at Gavin, then Drew, and back again to Gavin.

'I'm sorry, sis… I'll go n' get some warm soapy water. We didn't mean any harm like.' He felt really bad now. He liked Frayre, and now they would not be able to have such a nice catch up with her back home this weekend. *Honestly! Zarok…* In no time, Frayre's tanning booth was back to normal, unspeckled and shining. Her array of products were lined up neatly in a row and wiped down. The offending splobs were torn off the wall, taking the wallpaper with them however. Gavin beat a hasty retreat…Drew was sulking in their room and Zarok hiding under the bed.

'I was looking forward to going into town to get our tickets for the Monster Metallions, but all this crap this morning has taken the gloss off things a bit.'

'Zarok man…What were you thinking?!' cried Gavin.

'He's hardly done anything, Gav. She was freaking out over nothing! Just a few specks of tan here and there, and a couple of splobs…Anyone would think he had trashed her room! Even mum saw that it wasn't that bad. Her equipment had just been used a bit, that's all. That's what the blooming stuff's for– to be used!' exclaimed Drew bitterly.

'True…' remarked Gavin slowly, dragging a brush through his hair and chucking it to Drew. 'But…' Gavin looked a bit crestfallen.

'Look Zarok. We love our family, even though dad is a moron sometimes. And you simply can't go makin' trouble for us! This time it's turned out alright. But…But, no more splobs alright?!'

'What are we goin' to do about Zarok, Drew!' Gavin mouthed at his brother. But Zarok had clocked him.

'I'm sorry Gavin! I heard all of that. I didn't mean to make a mess. I was just unsure of how it worked and the thing came out in splurts. I thought someone was coming and I had to get rid of the tissue. I just got a bit carried away with lobbing splobs. I get bored in the day, and foolishly I was not thinking… They make a satisfying effect…'

'Well it ain't satisfying to me dad!' yelled Gavin, angry at Zarok for the first time.

'Oh no' whimpered Drew.

'What now?!' demanded Gavin, cupping his face in his hands.

'It's true Zarok. You gotta be no trouble to us! Just be safe, like you was when you sorted out the shed! I don't get how you can be cleaning up one minute and hanging on to ropes in a bell tower next, then chucking splobs. It doesn't make sense!'

'I am a boy, just like you Drew! I do the same sort of things!'

'Yes but you don't have to face the wrath of dad!' protested Drew, gazing sadly at his alien friend's vast, oceanic eyes.

'Or face cleaning off another splob!' groaned Gavin, stabbing at a milky, parched, dried splob (that he had just espied) with a pencil.

That afternoon, the boys went into town, meeting Reubin on the way, and soon Terry and Greg were in tow. Greg was able to purchase a ticket too. The other boys tried to reserve theirs. Gavin and Drew explained all of the latest.

'I warned you!' chided Terry bluntly as they sat outside the shopping mall.

'I gotta go coz my boring auntie and uncle are coming this afternoon, but me and Lee got together on his computer and we've been sussing out what 'Black Eyed Kids' are about… and they're trouble! I tell ya, if he asks to borrow your phone, it's the end! That's the truth. That's wot it says!' ended Terry dramatically. 'You shouldn't trust him so easily!'

Greg grimaced a bit. Terry was usually up for a laugh and they were generally on the same page, but not right now they weren't.

'He's not done anything awful, Terry! Get real!'

'Yeah, take a chill pill, Tez-face,' grunted Gavin in a huff.

Later that evening, Frayre and Gavin made up. She was a lively, spirited girl and her stories were good ones. She was quick to have a temper but didn't hold a grudge for long. Having invited them in, the children were now welcome in her room and were lounging around on her wide and comfy bed.

'In fact Gav, you've given me an idea! We've got to make a theatre set at college, and it's got to be funky. We've not got long to do it. I'm going to paint it bright purple and hurl some white and coloured 'splobs' at it until the backdrop's covered with them. I bet it will look really good with the lights shining on it!' Frayre smiled happily, stroking Billie's hair who was sitting on her lap. Then Billie blurted out…

'Gavin didn't chuck the splobs anyway. His new friend did.' *Bombshell!*

Drew and Gavin gaped at each other in horror. But Frayre didn't flinch.

'Yes I'm sure their mates put them up to it!' she laughed, before rattling on. 'Now this is a production we are aiming to put on at Christmas…' She explained it to them whilst rummaging around for her papers and finally producing a script. 'You would like it! It's a lovely story called 'The Silver Sword'. So listen up and I'll read some of it to you. I need to practice my lines for it too, so I will test you afterwards! Hopefully, you Gavin, Drew and Billie can come and see it once we are all rehearsed.' She launched into the story and the three of them listened intently, transported by the words. Except there wasn't only three of them… An alien called Zarok was stood in the hall, in the shadows, listening carefully with his exceptional hearing. And he too was captivated by the soulful tale.

CHAPTER SIX
SOME FANTASTIC NEWS!

It was Monday morning. Zarok was given strict orders to stay in the boy's room and remember that he was the 'deepest and darkest secret', as Drew had put it. This morning, Gavin and Drew were to walk Billie to school with them.

'Hurry up!' ordered Drew as Billie was dragging her feet across the pavement. But it was not because he was afraid in anyway of missing the school bell, and thus be late, but rather because he had spotted Terry n' Greg at the bus stop.

Drew left Gavin's side and sprinted up to meet his friends.

'Hiya Greg!' hailed Drew, greeting his friend by way of a light punch to his chest.

'Hiya,' grinned Greg.

'Alright buddy? How's Zarok?!' asked Terry intrigued.

'That's what we gotta talk about to you two. At lunchtime let's go to the library early, so we can get time on the computers. We'll check out Black Eyed Kids!'

Gavin strolled up, catching the last bit.

'Wotcha Greg! Wotcha Terry! How was your auntie?'

'Don't even go there,' replied Terry, pulling a face of disgust. Gavin went on, 'We're gonna do the same. Me, Reubin, Lee and Raj are heading for the library at lunch to find out about er...' He cast his head down to Billie who was looking up at him. 'To find out about frogs in their native habitat,' he ended uncertainly.

'Eh?' queried the others, slow to cotton on.

'Oh!' they realised, nodding ferociously.

But Gavin, Billie and Drew were already walking on, Drew waving back to his buddies.

'Catch you in school!' he yelled. The three children had each been given a chocolate biscuit and a pear for their breaktime. Gavin and Drew procured theirs and began munching simultaneously.

'Did you have breakfast?' asked Billie sounding concerned.

'Yep!' answered Drew heartily.

'Then why are you eating your breaktime snack?' demanded Billie.

'Coz I'm taking my break now.'

'But it's not breaktime yet,' persisted Billie.

'I'll take yours for later then,' plumped Drew. Billie thought about this for a bit, took a breath, and then kept quiet. The three now turned up the speed and soon Drew and Gavin were entering their favourite sweetshop near the school. They spent fifty pence each on dubious looking confections while Billie waited outside. Each of them had a bag of jelly zombies that oozed strawberry blood when you bit into them. In addition they'd purchased mega-popping candy to confuse the science teacher.

'Umm… You're not allowed!' gasped Billie.

'Shup! Don't tell mum or else,' snapped Gavin.

'See you two's later then,' called Gavin. The threesome had crossed the road and now split up towards their various school entrances.

Both Gavin and Drew found out they had an assembly that morning and took the news appreciatively. Neither were at their best on a Monday morning and the assembly meant that lessons were considerably shorter. Well, they always hoped they would be, but in truth, it didn't make that much difference. So it was a surprise when the form tutors told them it was a 'special assembly.' Unusually, Greg had been sent to join the assembly on the other side. All the children involved in the schools Cultural Awareness Day would be rewarded with book vouchers. Naturally Greg was chuffed to be joining his mates and settled himself next to them, much to their surprise. It would improve a 'special assembly' which to them meant a very long one...

'That sounds hopeful' whispered Gavin to Reubin gleefully. 'I could do with a snooze. Wake me up when it's over!' Reubin sniggered, 'No, you, me!' Soon Gavin, Reubin, Lee and Raj were all sat next to each other. Being still new to the lower secondary school, they were not old enough for chairs. Miss Hope, the maths teacher, eyed the four suspiciously, wondering whether to split them up in advance. They hadn't done anything disruptive yet, so she decided to just keep an eye on them.

Soon Mr Baldwin, a.k.a. 'Baldy', had taken the floor and cast his eyes blearily around the rows of faces.

'Today is a very special assembly...' he began unconvincingly. But Raj nudged Gavin with a hopeful expression. (The boys would communicate for the next half hour or so by pulling faces.)

'First, thank you to all the pupils who contributed to our Cultural Awareness Day. None of you had to contribute, but please don't put your name down to bring something if you're not committed. Apart from that, it was a success.'

'Indeed,' sniffed Miss Hope. 'We were missing beetroot soup, spaghetti hoops, and haggis and fufu from the menu, which was a disappointment.'

'Greg was meant to bring the fufu n' haggis, but he eats at Chick'n Nugget Central!' chortled a club enemy named Diggory.

Greg grimaced. They were cultural dishes of his that he liked, but he rarely ate them. It was true that Greg and his guardian did often eat chicken nuggets (as did most of the schoolchildren.) He wished he'd never signed up to bring in haggis and fufu. He'd been cajoled into it, as if it were a favour to him, but it wasn't. He'd forgot… His mates were annoyed on his behalf. They'd get Diggory back for this. But what about Miss Hope, would she?

'Out!' she bellowed at Diggory, as she hadn't meant anyone to be singled out.

Mr Baldwin had momentarily closed his eyes (hungrily recalling that spread.)

'Just coz that ponce brought in quinoa n' heritage tomatoes,' mocked Reubin audibly. Miss Hope tried not to smile, while Mr Baldwin looked around expectantly.

'Ahem! Today is a very special assembly since one of our patrons has died, leaving us with…' The teachers who stood around the perimeters of the assembly hall stifled giggles, hurriedly disguising them as sniffs into their hankies. Mr Baldwin looked humbled.

'Ahem!' he began for the third time.

'Sadly one of our dearly beloved patrons, so devoted to our schools in Higglesdon Wick, has passed away…' None of the assembled looked remotely moved.

'He leaves us with a most generous financial dividend…' Again, the teachers began to smirk, spluttering into their hankies. The children didn't understand why. The truth was that Mr Baldwin's speeches were often delivered badly or monotonously. He looked around blankly, visibly dumbfounded.

'Hum! He leaves us with the fondest memories! We are all indebted to his gracious interest in our school's development.'

'Who?!' called out a twelve-year-old boy named Gideon (another club enemy.)

'No calling out boy! He, that is, the right honourable Lord Chest-of-Cash, I mean, Lord Henley Chester Cass...has before his final resting place, God bless the man, seen fit to grant our noble school a substantial fund! May the good man rest in peace! It was thanks to Lord Cash, er Cass... that we are able to derive the utmost benefit from our gym. Last year, he funded state-of the-art gym equipment for us to enjoy. He leaves us with an outstanding sum of money, to which end he requires us to spend it with one of his last wishes.'

'Hurrah for Lord Cash!' Reubin shouted suddenly, concerned that a round of applause was necessary.

'No calling out, I said! Was that you, Reubin? Since I have already stipulated that no pupil should interrupt proceedings, it is doubtful whether you will be party to some of the benefits in store. Unless some exceptional behaviour from you overturns my decision! Let this be a lesson to all of you, because your best behaviour is certainly essential if you are to benefit from the opportunities to be allocated you! Lord Henley Chester Cass was an altruistic man. Having served in the army from...'

At this bit, most of the assembly gathered zoned out...

'Blah, blah and double blah...' whispered Gavin to Reubin. Mr Baldwin swooped down on Gavin like a hawk upon its prey.

'That goes for you too Gavin!' admonished the flint-eyed Head. And yet, ten minutes later, most of the pupils became alert to the speech.

'One of the things that Lord Cass was passionate about was that all pupils should be granted equal opportunities, regardless of background! We, here at Higglesdon Wick, are proud of our constitution that, as a long-standing comprehensive, we welcome pupils from the financially privileged to the less privileged and from all...'

'Yeah, like from 'benefits trousers' to toffee-nose Tony!' cut in Gideon enthusiastically.

'Out!' hollered Mr Baldwin, motioning to Miss Hope to eject him.

'He also felt strongly that school trips, including one's abroad, are an integral opportunity that all school children should experience as part of the curriculum! In that case, we are fortunate that, regardless of pupils' family finances, funds will be allocated across four classes per year to provide for this option.'

Finally, a frenzy of applause and 'Hoorays' broke out! It was as if this stagnant assembly hall had suddenly woken up, such was the eruption! Even Baldy managed a rare, toothy smile and a chuckle. He waited for the cheers to die down. The staff were smiling rapturously and clapping like mad.

'Many of you have brothers and sisters in the lower school. Those in the two highest years at Higglesdon Wick Primary will also be given the opportunity to go abroad, and are today listening to a similar assembly given by Mrs Jacobs. The children were now fidgeting. It was hot in the hall, but for once, they dared not stir or stare out of the huge windows looking onto the field. They were agog to hear more.

'At Higglesdon Wick we do not believe you should get something for nothing. We need to feel that you have earned it! Considering what you could be getting, this is not a big ask! Therefore, for the duration of the time leading up to the trip, you will be given a slip to record your attendance, and on the other side of it is a space for 'merit stamps' and 'comments' for exceptional achievements. Losing it is not an option! You will need to have these completed in order to be selected. De-merits, such as those that Gideon, Reubin and Gavin have just earned, could rule you out and *are* going to be taken seriously!'

'He does go on and on doesn't he...Where are we going then?' rasped Raj.

'Shhh...' went Gavin, looking down now.

'Do you think the children could find out where they could be going Mr Baldwin?' enquired Mr Anderson, trying to speed up proceedings.

'Ahem! Yes, indeed! From now on, let us go about our autumn term with renewed gusto. If we see litter lying in the playground, let us induce a community spirit in each other and jolly well pick it up and place it in the bins provided! Let us extend kindness to a lonely pupil during break. Let us choose to opt for homework club, instead of leaving school as early as possible!'

'Mr Baldwin? Let me just clarify here – Football Club!' expressed Mr Ball zealously, pointing to the field outside with an almost accusing finger.

'Indeed! Extra-curricular activities are essential and a thirst for knowledge too, if we are to explore the wonders of the globe, travelling so far afield...'

Now it was Lee who put his hand up.

'Yes Lee. That's the way!'

'Mr Baldwin. Please excuse me, but we are dying to know where we could be going?!'

'America, my boy! Lord Chester Cass loved America and was an ardent traveller and explorer! He wished nothing other than to instil that spirit of exploration in all of you. Therefore, some of you will be going to New York and others to different

States. Those of you who like hiking adventures can go to Utah, for example. Yet our staff considered you could do a project on wherever you want in America. It can be a group or personal project!'

'You will be expected to do a presentation on it, so we can all learn and open our eyes to the United States!' added Miss Hope. Mr Anderson nodded enthusiastically as he seemingly met with all the pupils' eyes at once.

'Upon that premise, your class teacher and you as a class may inject some input as to where you want to go. You actually have an opportunity to choose for yourselves and possibly sway our opinions!' Another cheer went up as a deliriously excited lower secondary school could hardly contain their excitement.

'Any questions?!'asked the Head.

'How long, Sir?'

'In six to eight weeks' time. Next?'

'Which years are going?' asked a wide-eyed Raj.

'The first four years, but I predict that a class worth of stragglers who have not earned the opportunity will be left behind! So mark my words!'

Finally, the assembly was over and most of the children filed out straight into the playground. It had gone on for so long, it was too late to begin the first part of the morning's lessons; just as Miss Hope had expected and endeavoured to avoid. So Reubin, Lee, Raj and Gavin grabbed a hot blackcurrant from the canteen. That always went down well at breaktime thought Gavin, as he munched thoughtfully on his apple. Then, the four of them took off to a favoured venue–behind the cycle sheds. A few older spotty looking youths had made it there first, skulking moodily and dragging on a cigarette, which they passed until half of it was torched orange.

'Sod off!' growled one unceremoniously.

'You won't be going to the USA if you're not careful!' reasoned Lee bravely.

'I won't, will I? Well you little squirt…'

'OK, OK!' soothed Gavin. 'We're going! We just had something to discuss…' Beating a hasty retreat, the boys took off to the back of the changing rooms instead. *Good. Noone was there!*

'Any of you's thinkin' wot I'm thinking?' mused Gavin aloud.

'Course! We got a chance to get Zarok back home!' breathed Lee excitedly.

'Oh *zeen*! Not that much of a chance,' put in Reubin wearily.

'That's coz you messed up, and might not be going! S'alright for you to say!'

'You got to buck up and not annoy the teachers, Reub. It wouldn't be the same if you didn't go!'

'Yep! We gotta hold a meeting of the Dogs and come up with a plan as to how we can get Zarok to America! It's too good to be true. It's… It's fate! It's serintripidy!' embellished Gavin gleefully.

'It's called 'serendipity', corrected Lee.

'Exactly. That!' clinched Gavin.

Over in the precincts of Higglesdon Wick Primary School, which was older and more rickety than the secondary school, similar proceedings had taken place. However, they had been delivered more succinctly and pleasantly by the headmistress, Mrs Jacobs. She was all for such opportunities that could make her school a happier place. It would also make her school life a lot less hectic for a few weeks… Many of the staff would be signed up for the USA trips too. The younger children were bubbling over with excitement. The only possible hitches would be if their parents were against them going abroad (and so far away too.) However, the unmissable opportunity was there. And not only that, the news was sure to travel to the rival grammar school, Higglesdon Wick High, and their Head would be as envious as hell. They would also be indignant as they had expected that Chester Cass's ample fortune would find its way into the kitty of their governing body, but Lord Cass had left them nothing but a new set of goalposts.

'Well, I enjoyed that assembly for once!' stated Drew who suddenly burst into a tribal wardance, as he perceived it. Terry n' Greg joined in, adding some whoops for effect.

'Yay!' whooped Greg when they had finished by linking arms and whirling around at breakneck speed. Dizzy, Terry fell over and they all stopped abruptly.

'You alright Tezza?'

'Yeah, I shouted for you to stop though! Brilliant news innit?!' A chorus broke out…

'We're going to AMERICA! La la LA LA AMERICA! La lalalala AMERICA!' This ditty went on as tunelessly as could be rendered, until they fell about laughing. When they had finished, their sides aching from shouting, Drew stopped short.

'Zarok! We can take Zarok home!'

'Why? He's only just got here dups!' insisted Greg perplexed.

'How?' said Terry simply.

'Where there's a will there's a way…' answered Drew dreamily.

Back at Gavin's secondary school, he and his friends piled into the lunch hall after their lessons in French and history were over.

'Lunch ain't half bad yana!' enthused Reubin.

'Fish n' chips– lovely!' seconded Lee.

'It's turning out to be a badass day. I vote we all go sit next to Anderson and get in his good books. Especially coz of you Reubin.' The boys filled their trays with a banana split for pudding and plonked themselves around the table where Mr Anderson sat.

'Are you coming on the trip, Sir?'

'Wouldn't miss it for the world!' smiled Mr Anderson. 'It's funny! Gavin and I were talking about the USA only the other day.'

'Well Sir. Me, Lee, Raj and Reubin are going to the library straight after lunch to find out things about America!'

'Good! I'm very glad to hear it! Personally, I think our Head was a bit hard on Reubin. I know you were only initiating the spirit of the occasion, but you must excel now, Reubin! Mr Baldwin, once he has an idea in his head, he's like a dog with a bone!'

The boys laughed. Anderson was a bit of a sport. In fact, the boys were now enthusiastic to start on their projects, but they knew they needed to swot up on Zarok first!

Once the boys had finished lunch, they raced into the library, where they were met with a sea of enthusiasts who were anxious to start on 'Project America'.

'Drat…Didn't think of this,' groaned Gavin seeing the seats filled, as umpteen pupils waited for the computer. Gavin was not a bully, but presently, he was a boy with a mission. At once, he espied a weedy looking first year on the last computer.

'You want any help with that? Let me sit down and sort it, it can be a bit slow!' offered Gavin anxiously through gritted teeth.

'No thank you! I'm a whiz with computers and can mend them myself and even build them.'

'He's a neek and a half,' mouthed Reubin meanly.

'Hey! I'm a neek too, so watch it!' said Lee offended. Gavin then tried plan B.

'Well if you are so clever then, you'll know they are giving away seconds of banana split with ice cream in the dinner hall!' said Gavin, pleased with how he was thinking on his feet. The weedy boy faltered. He was caving in.

'Alright then. You take my spot and look after it until I've finished my seconds! Thanks…Give me my place as soon as I come back!' finished the boy before racing off.

'Unfortunately, he didn't have time to hear my answer, which was going to be a *no…*' Gavin winked to the others and shook his head with a wry smile.

'Right, 'Black Eyed Kids!' He started searching for it and the boys brought two seats over to share.

'*Lond up dil ting*' said Reubin, rubbing his hands importantly, which roughly meant 'to disclose someone's business'. Gavin knew all the slang anyway.

'Yep! It's that alright bruv!' echoed Gavin.

'How come you didn't use your brother Alex's PC?' asked Lee.

'Coz like you, he's always on it. Anyway, risky! He might find what we've been on and he's inquisitive too. Me n' Drew could try the once though.' Soon there was a page up on assorted stories about *Black Eyed Kids*. The boys read them one by one.

'Look at this! *Marcia and Chuck from Texas had a ring at their doorbell late at night. They opened it partially to see two kids begging to use their phone! They said they needed to call home! Marcia felt a lurch in her stomach…She knew something didn't add up, and then the cat started wailing… Something told her not to open that door, but she was being compelled to open it, so much so, it was hard to fight it!'*

'Wow! Go on!' urged Raj. But now there was an interruption. Unnoticed, Gideon had sauntered over with his gang and was extending his arms around the boys back, as if in a matey manner, but it was a fake show as both sets of boys hated one another as a matter of course.

'We know what yer doing!' sang Gideon's mate, Diggory.

'Black Eyed Kids, aye? I wonder if me n' Dig are gonna tell Baldy that your project is bogus and you're not taking this assignment seriously!' mocked Gideon, attempting to put on the headmaster's voice. Montgomery and his other mate, Josh, guffawed appreciatively at their leader's pop at the rivals.

'Big ups Gid,' slurred Josh, with each of his arms round a pal's shoulder.

'Like you're gonna be going after tryin' to be centre of attention in assembly!' fired back Gavin blandly, without turning around.

'Geroff my back posho!' snarled Reubin irritably, pushing Montgomery away.

'Ah yes, I might catch your bad taste in coats…' sneered Montgomery.

'Ha ha…! That's so funny! Like we all don't have to wear blazers! We all got da same get up, man!'

Lee was feeling annoyed. He wanted to get on!

'Get lost, Gideon!' snarled Lee (uncharacteristically) irritably, trying to toss Diggory off of his arm.

'Dogs of Hell!' That's a rubbish name for a club. You'll never guess ours! It's proper top secret as we change our name every week!'

'I bet it's 'Trainspotters United' quipped Raj, on form. Then Gavin supplied, 'Doesn't matter what your name is. We already know you do *nothing* exciting and your stupid headquarters is your Granny's living room!' He made the action of being sick, whereby Reubin laughed, while at the same time hoisting up his shoulders to look threatening. Gideon took a step forward and they engaged in a face-off. Then, there was another interruption.

The weedy boy, who was, in fact, a nice and very interesting lad, came back.

'Thanks for looking after my place!' he said smiling. 'There was no pudding though?!'

'You don't say?' gasped Gavin in mock surprise.

'Get lost!' snubbed Reubin bluntly, but he didn't need to block the way, thanks to Gideon.

Gideon moved, however, saying 'Be my guest little boy! Come on Gavin! Give Norbert his place back now or he might tell his mummy. And he's probably booked it through the nice librarian. And you sure as hell haven't!' Norbert, rather naively, was trying to squeeze in.

'Give me my place back!' he cried. 'I was doing my maths… You said…'

'I said there was seconds of banana split. You're the banana and it's time for you to split!' Gavin gave him a firm nudge, while Gideon's clan guffawed again.

'Don't laugh at his jokes you scabs! He's the enemy and he ain't funny!' snapped Gideon.

'Get LOST! *Don't get mi ig!*' tried Reubin again, shoving Gideon so hard that he ran backwards.

Then the librarian came over…

'OK boys. Enough! The library is a quiet place for study. Both of you, Gideon and Reubin, are going to get a black mark. Hand me your slips please, and be aware that this could go against you for the USA trip.'

'We're gonna get you outside Gideon, you pillock!' snarled Gavin. The boys left the library dejected. At this rate, there was no way Reubin would be going to America! They would have to come up with something, plus teach Gideon and his moronic gang a lesson!

Meanwhile, back in the primary school, proceedings were going more successfully. Gavin hadn't thought that capable Drew, Terry n' Greg would all be on it too. They had learnt quite a bit and printed some A4s off, plus taken notes. They were glad to have more info on Zarok. The problem was, they didn't believe the half of it. It was clear that Zarok was a good alien, and as Zarok had said, Black Eyed Kids certainly had a bad reputation! They also found that Zarok was supposed to be a kind of insect with huge suckers. As far as they could tell, he wasn't in possession of such sucking pipes on either side of his head. Black Eyed Kids were supposed to feed on energy or something…

'They are the energy scavengers of the universe, sort of feeding on it!' deduced Greg.

'But he eats sweet potato and your mum's cactus…' objected Terry.

'We got all of this, and we will have to go through it and draw our own conclusions!' concluded Drew. Feeling like a detective, he then turned up his collar for effect.

'And, of course, learn from the horse's mouth by asking Zarok! I mean he's kept a bit quiet about himself, hasn't he?' Terry had a point.

'Me and Gav will ask our brother Alex if we can use his PC. But we will just look at habitat. Where they live and things…

You and Greg can look more in depth on *Black Eyed Kids* at home…'

'But we just been doing that for ages! I'm gonna be playing 'Role of War Duties' when I get in!' said Terry firmly.

'Yeah? We need to fathom out *where* we should coax the teacher to go in America? So we can get Zarok back…That's most important! We didn't look at the Devil's Highway yet!'

Terry looked as if his blood had run cold. 'We won't want to go there, will we?' He shivered a little for effect.

'Of course! Sounds like it's the rad'ist stomping ground for us Dogs of Hell! You were sayin' it was gonna be one hell of a ride the other day!' recalled Drew.

'Yeah, Dogs of Hell's paradise!' seconded Greg, nudging his friend.

'All I'm sayin' is ask Zarok where e' really comes from– just sayin'?!' quibbled Terry, holding his hands up in defence.

The boys then split as they neared the bus stop, and made for home. Meanwhile, back outside the school gates, Gideon, Gavin, Reubin and Montgomery were slugging the hell out of each other with their bags. Finally, Montgomery's bag strap broke as he was wielding it around. Swiftly, Raj grabbed it from the ground and emptied the contents into a puddle. A chase resumed up the road in the direction of the bus stop. But the Dogs of Hell, who were faster runners than their rivals, got on the bus first, and the doors slammed behind Gideon's gang who gaped at them in hapless fury.

'Thanks!' said Gavin to the bus driver, while the others stuck their fingers up and pulled grotesque faces at the enemy out the window.

'Fine! Anytime! Those four are a blessed nuisance.' *A pretty good end to a school day*, considered the boys, though the day itself was not over and there was a bit of a problem. In all the scuffle and excitement, Lee and Raj were on the wrong bus. Worse still, the direction it was heading in was out of their way for getting back!

'Drat!' said Lee, as he stood by the doorway, waiting for Raj to join him.

'O-M-Geee!' exclaimed Lee. No reinforcements if we bump into Gideon, Diggory and Posho on the way back. Least the bus driver is on our side.'

'Holy-Moley…' mumbled Raj. *At least they were no longer on open territory.* Open combat wasn't an option if they were going to be picked off later!

***

In the evening, Brian had something to tell Miriam. 'I found a leaflet lying around the house. I believe it fell out of the paper the other day. Well, here's the thing. It reminded me that the building down the road, which houses people with various compulsive disorders, need help with decorating. Geoff read in the paper that they've had their funding cut to the bone. I believe they do an excellent job in restoring folk with various issues back to health. So we are going to chip in and volunteer with a team, going in for two weekends to paint and decorate. You know, do me bit!'

'That's really good of you, Brian! And after that you can start on ours!' she joked, while at the same time meaning it… It seemed that Drew's leaflet had found its way into his dad's hands after all. But not with quite the result that he'd anticipated!

***

CHAPTER SEVEN
REVENGE PLANNED ON HIGGLESDON WICK HIGH

he Mason boys could hardly wait to tell Zarok the news. They burst in the door of twenty-four Cherry Tree Lane, and totally forgetting themselves, shouted, 'Hey ZAROK!!' in unison. Then the pair clamped their hands over their mouths, as if to cover up their outburst, and changed gear completely by creeping stealthily towards the stairs.

'Who you boys shouting for? What's Zarok?' demanded a shrewd-eyed dame, in a floral apron. It was Miriam's home help, Mrs Beak, who was approaching them. The boy's mum hired her every other week to sort out the house. Mrs Beak was not only a very thorough home help, she was also the nosiest neighbour in the district. Drew and Gavin's hearts sank. They had forgotten about her. The old fogey, as they thought of her, could give the whole game away! Her corpulent personage now stood blocking the foot of the stairs, and worse still, Zarok had obediently come running, arriving at the top of the stairs. Roji the dog was barking ferociously, sensing an atmosphere.

Drew, who was standing behind Gavin with his hands outstretched, started to utter moans of: 'Where doth thee go yonder Zaroke?'

Mrs Beak looked startled.

'He's practising his part for a Russian play. It's gone to his head,' explained Gavin squarely to Mrs Beak. He was impressed with his brothers acting skills.

'Whatever you're practising, I need to be cleaning your room next!' Zarok had made a speedy disappearance, and at lightning speed, started to tidy it up.

'No, I don't think so!' remonstrated Gavin.

'Don't tell mum about our play, Mrs Beak. It's going to be a surprise. Why don't you take a break and Drew will make you a nice cup of tea.'

'Oooh… That does sound good, Gavin. But I must first see to your room, dear. Your mum doesn't pay me to be idle.' And with that, she grabbed a broom and brandished it over her shoulder, like a militant going into battle.

'Stop her! Get Roji to jump her!' gasped Drew.

'I can't. Look at her! She just does as she pleases in our house!'

Powerless to stop the determined Mrs Beak, Drew and Gavin dolefully sloped behind her to their room. Peering around the door, she scoured the walls and bed and carpet and bedside tables with laser-like eyes. Then she let out a loud, 'Hurrumph!'

'Well stone the crows!' she said finally. I must say this room is spic and span. I almost didn't recognise it, Gavin and Drew. That does make a nice change! Since there is nothing more for me to do I will take you up on that cuppa.' Mrs Beak made herself comfortable with a magazine in the Mason's front room.

'It's got to be done Drew. *We gotta get rid of her!* Gavin swapped the bowl of sugar for salt, brought a tray in, and then fled! Before long there was a loud cry of 'Mercy me! Eugh!' A slam of the door followed and Mrs Beak was gone!

'But for how long…' moaned Gavin.

As soon as Gavin and Drew had got to their room, there was a knock at their bedroom window. Reubin's face appeared, and Drew went to pull up the sash.

'I gotta tell you, my mum and your mum's made friends with Posho's mum, and the bad news is that they're coming round to yours and bringing *HIM* with them!' he informed them testily as he pulled himself in. *'Hear mi, bruv!'*

'We haven't got time to waste on that! Look! We gotta tell Zarok! Zarok, you'll never guess what. Oh, thanks so much for cleaning our bedroom by the way! You saved us!' Reubin was lying full length on Drew's bed. All of the boys had whipped their shoes off and the room now stank to high heaven! So it hardly *smelt* clean anymore!

'Zarok! Our schools are going to America! You know what that means, don't you? That we might get half a chance to get you back home! Not that we want you to go!' A sad look crept over the alien's features, his huge opaque eyes looking even more soulful than usual, while he twiddled his long tapering fingers.

'Kind Gavin. It seems so near and yet so far. First off, I may not be accepted in America. My time on the Devil's Highway proved that the lifestyle was not for me. Secondly, how on earth will you manage to take me with you and your class?! I don't even attend Higglesdon Wick!'

Gavin glared at his favourite poster of the Monster Metallions as if his musical heroes could give him an answer.

Drew and Reubin looked downcast as they gazed at Zarok. But Gavin ignored the obvious.

'I thought you wanted to go home, Zarok! Don't worry about logistics. We will find a way!' In a way, the Monster Metallions had given him hope.

'First of all, we're all going to the concert at the end of the week! That is our first outing together in public to test the waters! Then, me and Drew, no me and Reubin, will take you to our school and enrol you! That will be testing things further. We will see how long we can keep you there!'

Zarok didn't want to be rude and argue, after all, he was Gavin's guest and it was better to go with the flow. His tense features relaxed and he revealed a tiny slither of razor teeth in a cheeky grin.

'Yay! That's the spirit Zarok! That's how we like you, game for anything.' Then…

'Drew! Gavin! Come down for some dinner! We have a visitor for you from your school!' It was Gavin and Drew's mum. *Oh no! Reubin must have been spot on* thought Gavin. Gavin and Drew traipsed in.

'Hullo Honour,' Drew greeted Reubin's mum.

'Hi mum. Hi Honour!' said Gavin, ignoring Montgomery's mum. Undeterred, Miriam said: 'This is Emilline and her son, who attends Higglesdon Wick. You may say 'hello' to them too boys! Now let's all go have a bite to eat.'

'*Betta belly buss dan good food waste!* Isn't Reubin here?' queried Honour.

'Yes,' said Drew while Gavin said, 'No!' Reubin's mum looked perplexed.

'I will go up and see if he's there, Honour!' soothed Miriam embarrassed.

'No!' cried Drew.

'What on earth is going on?' Gavin raced upstairs to haul Reubin downstairs. He came and sat down, acknowledging his mum and saying 'hello' to Miriam. The boys glowered at Montgomery.

'Of course, I would have preferred Montgomery to attend Higglesdon Wick High, but sadly, in the end, my husband Brad and I decided to send him to the comprehensive,' sighed Emilline, tucking into a steaming Ghanaian feast that Miriam and Honour had put together at their cookery class.

'Was that because he had to pass a stiff exam to get in?' enquired Miriam innocently.

'Of course not! Montgomery is extremely bright, aren't you Monty?! No, it was oversubscribed!'

'Oversubscribed with twots,' murmured Gavin under his breath.

'Gavin!' His mum pulled him up sharply.

'He doesn't like him!' pointed out Billie helpfully.

'So I take it you boys know each other!' exclaimed Emilline brightly.

'Yes,' agreed Gavin, raising his eyebrows to heaven.

'So do you do sports together? You all get on well I take it?' tried Emilline.

'No, we don't!' answered Reubin blankly. Montgomery pulled a face of repugnance at him over the dinner table.

'Don't you like your food, Monty?' asked Miriam concerned.

'Oh yes, I do Mrs Mason. This stew is delicious! It's just, I was thinking… I suddenly remembered how Mr Baldwin called out poor Gavin in assembly. Although we haven't had the chance to get to know each other, I do hope it means that Gavin won't be struck off the USA trip.'

'Is that so Gavin?! Words later! I must say, it's the first I've heard of the USA trip!'

'I have heard of it. In fact, Higglesdon High received no funding whatsoever from Lord Chester Cass,' sniffed Emilline. 'Not that Brad and I would need funding for a school trip on our income!'

'Really!' remarked Honour, looking surprised. She noted that Emilline could hungrily put away the food. *'Pompasetting...' murmured* Honour, one eyebrow raised. It meant 'showing off!'

'Don't put your handbag on the floor, it will make you poor my dear!' advised Honour with a wink. Emilline looked outraged. She picked it up and put it back down again.

'That's a Caribbean custom, well not custom, but saying,' smiled Miriam.

'I do believe there is bad blood between Higglesdon Wick Comprehensive and High,' revealed Emilline with a sniff. 'My cousin attended Higglesdon High before going on to university and a stellar career as a lawyer. I seem to recall that there was a theft. Strangely, it was Higglesdon Wick High that was accused of taking valuable documents and some priceless article of furniture. Something to do with workmen, I believe. The same two school heads, who have presided as headmasters for thirty years, have never made it up! The theft was never resolved, but I heard that a chair, which was said to have belonged to Henry VIII, remains an item of pride and joy at Higglesdon Wick High.'

'How interesting!' exclaimed Miriam, topping up everyone's fruit punch.

'Mercy! Fascinating!' seconded Honour, who had hoped that more would be said about their cooking extravaganza. *Some proper discussion about the dishes was in order.* But

Gavin had found it interesting. *Very interesting!* He had already decided to get to the bottom of this and use it in his favour. Montgomery could guess this and looked doleful.

'Er… Can we be excused mum? Homework! Loads of it! Good to see you Honour! Nice to see you Emilline and Posho, I mean Monty!' The boys dashed out before there was any come back.

'Pickney dem!' gasped Honour, with a throw of a manicured hand. As the ladies engaged in conversation, Montgomery became bored and glanced towards the door, only to see two fingers stuck up at him by way of goodbye!

Reubin had got out the fastest. He did not want to go home with his mum, but hang out with his friends for longer. This seemed to be OK anyway, as the ladies engaged in a long talk over supper, while Montgomery sat in the corner dejectedly doing his maths homework. When the boys arrived upstairs, they said to Zarok, 'Hey, Reubin's gonna chat to you, while we go and do a search on Alex's PC while he's out.'

'Don't worry. I got my phone and there's internet,' offered Reubin. 'What we lookin' at?'

'Check out that story that Posho's mum was on about! I have to be honest Zarok, the chances of me and Reubin going to USA could be slim. We've already been in trouble and are likely to be in some more, knowing our luck. Baldy has got it in for us! We wanna find out about that theft and return it to Baldy! Then, we will be in his good books forever!'

'Nice one bruv!' cheered on Drew, impressed by Gavin's idea (though unimpressed that he had been in trouble so soon!) Zarok leaned over to look at the mobile too, looking quite excited. He must have often been bored at home and so loved new dramas!

Soon the info was at their fingertips. 'Even Lee couldn't have found this quicker than us! Here look!' All the boys were bouncing excitedly on the bed.

'Stop that! I can't see!' yelled Gavin.

'Memba mi tell yu!' implored Reubin. 'Check this bredrin!' he went on.

'Here we are! Back in 1991, Higglesdon Wick underwent some refurbishment, including to the head's office, which was Baldy's! Seems dat Baldy had some special documents he hid behind an old painting. Oh, the painting was special too. Those documents were of all the mayor's endorsements to the school up to date and some important bursary paperwork, plus a decade's sports certificates from the sixties. *Pree!* Then there was that chair. A beautiful embellished yew chair, inlaid with pearl, said to have belonged to Henry the blooming VIII! Basically, Headmaster Herbert from the other school nicked the lot! All my days!' Reubin and Gavin gaped at one another as they took this in.

'How?' asked Zarok, feeling sorry for the boys' headmaster.

'Basically…' replied Gavin, skim reading, 'Basically, workmen in white overalls came in. They stripped the office and simply placed the items in the school dump. And then they went back to do the painting. Afterwards, they thought about it for a bit; then they decided to try sell it to the other school for a few extra bucks!'

'I bet it doesn't say that's what happened,' challenged Drew.

'No but I bet that's what did happen! You can tell! Whatever, Herbert has never given the items back, and apparently cheekily keeps them in his office to this day! He has said in the paper, the items are his and he acquired them fairly and paid for them!'

'We need a full-on meeting about this with the rest of the club,' cut in Reubin before stopping short. 'Shhhh! There's someone outside!'

'Damn! I thought I could hear scuffling,' hissed Drew. 'But it just didn't register!'

'Crap! It's him, Posho!' cried Gavin angrily, hurling himself at the door and running out into the corridor. A familiar boy's head stuck his head out from around the banister, saying: 'Don't worry, Mason! I heard everything! You wait 'til I tell Gid!' and with that he was gone. He joined his mum and they left the next minute.

Gavin came back red in the face, utterly broken.

'Crikey! How could I forget?! Forget that *he* was here, an enemy on our doorstep! A deadly enemy on *our* territory!'

'Yeah, man. *Im is bare wassy!*' groaned Reubin, fearing for Gavin.

'Do you think he heard Zarok, Gavin?!' simpered Drew, looking white in the face.

'How should I know!' raved Gavin. Too dejected to go on, the boys decided to call it a night. They were simply too shell shocked to speak anymore. Reubin went off to join his mum (via the staircase this time) to walk back home with her. Slapping his friend's backs affectionately, he consoled them, 'Don't worry! It'll be fine. We'll get 'em back tomorrow yana!'

The boys slept really well that night. Before that though, Gavin and Drew did the usual chatting to Zarok whilst snuggled up in their beds. Drew had brought up lots of sweet potato left over from the evening's dinner. Zarok was savouring it, eating out of some tin foil. They were all nice and full and felt a lot better. In the late evening, as Zarok talked, you could be forgiven for forgetting that he was an alien from another planet. In times like these, he seemed just like any other boy, although extra sensitive to everything.

'I will help you get those things back to your headmaster dudes. Tomorrow, if needs be!' offered Zarok with a twinkle in his eye.

***

The next day dawned. Drew and Gavin fled out the door with a mission to accomplish. They needed, of course, to find out what Montgomery knew! Had he heard Zarok speak?! He should have told his mum to get Posho to leave early, that he hated him! Terry n' Greg were picked up on the way, and soon Reubin came running down the road from King Charles Street after them.

'Wah gwaan!' they greeted one another with friendly punches. Yesterday's events were discussed. The little gang of boys didn't say much, but they stepped on it that day. They knew Gideon's lot got to school early, as they were often dropped off by their folks. Gideon, Montgomery, Josh and Diggory were chatting by the school gates, and snickered together as their rivals appeared.

'Thanks for inviting me for dinner! It was lovely!' smiled Montgomery with a nasty smirk.

'You had loads of seconds of that pudding, didn't you? Coconut and mango island delight! Pity the others didn't get to have theirs…' added Gideon with a mock tear. Protective of his own domain, Gavin felt like he'd been invaded by a cat usurping his territory. He was practically hissing at them.

'Excuse me? *A who yu, man?!*' contested Reubin in Gavin's defence.

'You've got a shabby old carpet though!' their foe went on nastily. 'You could do with putting your lazy cleaner through her paces,' sneered Montgomery. Now Gavin was almost ready to spring like a cat. But, instead, he said coolly: 'What were you listening to, sneaking outside my room Posho?!'

'Ah now – well, let me see? Oh yes, I know. That's for me to know and you to find out!' clucked Montgomery, obviously thoroughly enjoying winding them up. But by now Lee had turned up, and without being seen, got behind Montgomery and took his arms behind his back.

'Come on, Montgomery. What did you hear or I won't let go.'

The Gideon gang then set upon Lee, tugging him off, while the Dogs of Hell, now feeling fearless, took this as the moment to steam in. It was close to turning into a full-on fight.

Soon, Montgomery was pinned against the tall black iron gates.

'Well? What did you hear us saying?' snarled Gavin.

'Tell im y' donk!' seconded Reubin who was backing Gavin in.

'Not telling you! Get off you prat! Teacher's coming!' Gavin didn't believe him.

He should have done. Suddenly, Miss Hope came striding up to the lot of them looking incensed. Meanwhile, Terry, Greg, Gideon and Josh were all bundling in a heap on the ground, trying to get the better of each other.

'This is totally unacceptable!' shrieked Miss Hope. 'Get off of each other and get up immediately!' Nine dusty dishevelled boys got up.

'You Drew, Terry and Greg. Get to your school, now! You are not allowed on these premises! As for you lot; you Gavin, Gideon and Reubin… I'm coming to expect trouble from you three.

Detention after school! And, of course, you will be coming to my office whereby you will receive demerits on your USA slips!' A crowd of giggling students had gathered around them...

'But I'm not late, Miss!' (Gavin did not want to lose face.)

'It's for your outrageous behaviour this morning! There is to be no fighting on these premises, and by the school gates too! Wait until Mr Baldwin hears of this!' And with that, Miss Hope strode off, brushing down her smart jacket as she went.

'Whew! She's in a bad mood!' said Gavin. Miss Hope turned round again. 'All of you– split!' The groups of boys, split! But as they did so, Montgomery couldn't resist turning around and singing...

'We know the Hell Dog's plans! Like to see you try and get Baldy's tack back from Higglesdon High!'

And Gideon added in a menacing tone, 'And we'll all be there waiting for you to make a mistake... Ha ha!'

But Gavin turned to Reubin and breathed a sigh of relief! 'Thank Goodness for that! It means they didn't hear Zarok!!'

'I told you it would be alright!' comforted Reubin, looking into his friend's familiar face and grinning broadly. 'Trust mi!'

'Zarok didn't say much, or anything then.'

'Come on. Let's get to class!'

CHAPTER EIGHT
REVENGE TAKES STRANGE SHAPE

The following morning, there was a strained silence as Drew, Gavin and Billie sat around the breakfast table, putting away their cereal and drinking their tea. Gavin had his eye on his mother who was reading a letter with a look of dismay. Too bad he hadn't had time to feed it to the dog.

'This is disappointing Gavin, a bad letter from school; from Mr Baldwin himself.' Gavin assumed an expression of outraged innocence while Miriam went on.

'Fighting!' she said matter of factly.

'Oh that… I'm sorry mum, but why did you bring Posho round? You know he's our enemy and nothing wrong would have happened if he hadn't come and spied on us.'

'What on earth are you talking about, and please don't call him Posho!'

'Why not? That's what he is,' volunteered Drew between noisy slurps of milk.

'He and his mum Emilline are very nice and, in fact, I have given her the details of that summer camp so he can…'

'OH NO!' shouted Drew before she could finish her sentence. 'How COULD you!' slapping his hand over his forehead for maximum effect.

'He doesn't like him…' whispered Billie helpfully. But Gavin was anxious not to get into the ins and outs, and upped and left the kitchen as soon as possible with Drew following suit. There were important plans to be made. In fact, they had already been made and tonight they were to be carrying them out! Zarok had been briefed that morning and was going to be in on them. In fact, he was going to be the main man.

Reubin was waiting outside the gate for Gavin. He looked impatient with his schoolbag slung over his shoulder and tie at half-mast.

'I thought you said you were gonna be here ten minutes early!' he fumed. 'I might as well have stayed in bed for ten yana!'

'Soz Reub, but my mum was half having a go at me!' explained Gavin rather untruthfully.

'He's been naughty and got into a fight,' said Billie bluntly. The boys ignored her. Meanwhile, Drew ran on to meet his besties, Terry n' Greg at the bus-stop. This morning they all took the bus together.

'Gwaan? You n' Gav got yer mobiles back yet?' was their greeting.

'Er…Well, we got one between us for now. And I tell ya, we're going to be needing them tonight!' Then Drew launched into the best-laid plans for that very evening. Greg and Terry were quieter than usual, taking it all in, and were stretched out at the back of the bus. Finally, Terry let out a long, 'Whoo…eee…!' And Greg said: 'You are joking aren't you? We're going to let Zarok into Herbert's office to ask for the booty? Is he going to wear a mask or what?'

'Zarok's up for it,' beamed Drew proudly.

'I bet he is alright,' agreed Greg, 'but all hell could be let loose! It's a high-risk operation as it is! One thing though. We'd better to do it asap before Gideon's gang gets grass of it dups.'

At lunchtime, a familiar clan of boys, including Gavin, Reubin, Raj and Lee, could be seen stationed outside the bicycle area.

'I think it's better we hold a serious meeting to do with a mission at our allotment!' stated Reubin, looking about him wildly.

'I don't think there's time for that,' said Raj gently, prompting Gavin to relay the evening's plans to the gang. Hands in his pockets, Gavin simply launched into it.

'This is what we're doing! You Lee, Raj, Drew and Terry n' Greg will be stationed at intervals around Higglesdon Wick High. Half the way round is Higglesdon Court. That's OK. Entrances covered, me and Reubin will climb over the fence or even walk straight in, we dunno yet – with Zarok!' The members gasped, looking dubiously at each other. Gavin went on.

'It's red-hot alert and you lot can't just be standing around exchanging texts! You gotta look out for Gideon, Diggory, Monty and Josh.'

'But if we stand around texting it looks natural and inconspicuous!' disputed Lee.

'One gold star award!' muttered Gavin sarcastically.

'We gotta communicate, but not overtly about events! Mobiles can be confiscated or nicked.'

'We'll use our codes,' affirmed Lee.

'What if we see Gideon and all?' queried Raj.

'Run for it, then reconvene, plus let us know, of course!' ordered Gavin, his eyes conveying intent. And this intent was unwavering. Much was at stake.

'We're all going to take up our places at quarter past six and… Here, pass us the papers, Reubin! Nice one, mate. This is a map so you know our positions! The second paper is a letter that we've done from Mr Herbert, apologising to Baldy. It says he wished he'd never stolen them items and how he'd been longing to give em' back and…'

'Let's look at that!' exclaimed Lee urgently, before grabbing it.

'You can't use that! Look at it… And it's not even typed!' he ranted. Sure enough, the letter was a mess with ink spots everywhere. Gavin had assumed that headmasters used fountain pens and he was not a dab hand at using them. It read:

'Dear Mr Baldwin Its been ages now since I nicked your speshal painting and took all your documents about the school cetificats. I am sorry I got your chair from henry the eaith and at last I am givin it back yours truly Mr Herbert. PS: I hop that due to your very clever studunts particully the nice boys that talked me round an showd me the error of my ways will benfit from that USA trip.

The boys cracked up laughing and Gavin went red, looking offended. Even Gavin's main man Reubin declared it 'bogus'. 'That's funny man! That's unreal bruv!' he said.

'I s'pose it's not that good' Gavin relented. 'I was tired that's all. Lee will type out a good one. Go on Lee, now!' Lee agreed and took off saying he would type it in such a way that the Head, Mr Herbert, need only sign it!

'Good on Lee, saving the day. It was so obvious it wasn't from Baldy!' sighed Raj incredulously.

'I don't see you doing any work laying out plans?!' scoffed a miffed Gavin. But, with all the boys' ears on the shrill school bell morbidly signalling the end of break, Gavin recovered himself, and as leader of the Dogs of Hell, gave his parting shot.

'Don't forget, quarter past six, check into your positions! Good luck! Laters!'

And with that the boys split, running off in different directions. There was time for them to meet up after school briefly, which this time included Greg, Terry and Drew. Here, they agreed they would tell their parents they were going to a school concert that evening, and it was true that there was one on. They hoped the short notice wouldn't mean they'd have to abort their plans.

With that in mind, Drew and Gavin picked up Billie and dropped into their mum's hairdressers, explaining how they needed to attend 'the concert' in good time. They also offered to do some shopping for her, which she was most pleased about, and then went to the supermarket before heading home. Gosh! They were a bit tired now!

But Zarok wasn't. He had spent all day perfecting his English accent, viewing the plans and revising how best he might carry them out. For example, should he spring himself upon Mr Herbert so as to scare him? Or should he pretend to be one of Higglesdon comprehensive's boys and try a charm offensive? And, if Herbert wasn't there – which hadn't occurred to any of the boys – should he just take the items and flee? Of course, he was dying to discuss all this with the club.

But alas, after a faint 'Hi Zarok!' the two boys crashed out on their beds for a good hour. It was quarter to six before Zarok was shoving Drew and Gavin, saying 'Come on Drew… Wake up Gav! It's time to go, dudes!'

'Thanks Zarok! Yes, indeed. It's time alright! You wearing your hoodie?' *Good it was getting darker.* The boys sped down Cherry Tree Lane which would take them to Apple Orchard Road. There was no time to wait for the bus! They were way too slow. Zarok was a fast runner and was easily beating them. Soon they arrived in Higglesdon Court and lay out on the grass for a moment or two to catch their breath. Suddenly, Reubin appeared, saying: 'Good you made it! Hi Zarok! Ready for this?' Then he added, rather ominously, 'You gotta get this bare right, or me and Gavin won't be able to get back into favour with Baldy, which will mean no USA for us, and we won't be able to get you back home!'

'Alright? Don't give him pressure, Reubin!' scolded Gavin, alarmed. Drew had split and run around the corner to take up his place on the western entrance of Higglesdon Wick High. In the distance, he could see Raj further up the road on the end. Or was it? Gavin had the phone so he couldn't tell.

The gates of Higglesdon Wick High were open but looked imposing. Whether or not they climbed over a lower wall on the East side of the building or walked in was irrelevant. They needed to know where the Head's office was. Reubin took the plunge and walked straight in. It was empty apart from a caretaker he could see in the distance. He walked quickly down the corridor immediately in front of him, as soon as the caretaker had turned a corner. After a couple of offices and one more saying 'Reception', he came to an office on the right hand side that was clearly marked 'Master Herbert.' *Well, that was easy!* Encouraged, Reubin got out, and went to meet his friends who were stationed outside. The three made their way into the grounds and then followed Reubin up a narrow path (which looked out of bounds) on the right hand side of the school.

'OK! I reckon his office is the fourth window along!' hissed Reubin.

'Now Zarok. *Check mi.* Me and Gav are going to help you up and in, then we'll sit on the wall here opposite for you. We might have to go over on the other side if needs be. Bossman!' he added amiably, slapping Zarok on the back. Zarok had pulled his black hoodie tight around his silvern visage, and they couldn't tell if he was nervous or not. Suddenly, the situation was all too real and intense.

'Well now, the window is open a tad,' noted Gavin. It was smallish and square.

'Do you think you can get into that Zarok?! We gotta hurry up before he goes home!'

'We don't know if he's in there yet,' said Zarok, betraying that he was indeed nervous!

'Don't play for time. Now you've got the letter he's gotta sign. We will count one, two, three, and then give you a leg up, Zarok. Don't screw it up, and I don't mean the letter!'

Duly, on the count of three, the pair hoisted Zarok up to the window. The alien was remarkably agile anyway and could have shinned up and in without their help. The next thing they knew, Zarok was sat perched up on the window with his legs hanging in. A portly man with a thickset head, that looked as though it had been modelled out of pork, glanced up in astonishment as he pulled at a pair of spectacles.

'Well I never!' he muttered finally. Zarok braced himself…

'What do you think you're playing at boy?!' demanded Mr Herbert, recovering his characteristic ferociousness.

There was something a bit different about this boy considered Master Herbert. Certainly, he didn't recognise him as a pupil from Higglesdon Wick High.

'Come down from there immediately so that I can see you!' the staunch man bellowed suddenly, standing up to get a better view. Zarok could see the man's eyes searching through the glass in the door, and instinctively he knew that it could be seconds before the caretaker was alerted. Zarok had to find a way to ensure that Mr Herbert kept his eyes and attention on him!'

'With pleasure, I will come down, Sir. I have dealings with you that are long overdue!'

'L-long overdue!' spluttered the formidable headmaster, indignant with rage.

Zarok went and stood in front of the door. (Suddenly Gavin's face jumped halfway up the window, mouthing 'HURRY UP!' before disappearing.

'I've come for the booty, Mister!' announced Zarok swiftly.

'B-booty?! The insolence of it!' bawled Mr Herbert.

'Yes indeed, Sir. Booty belonging to Mr Baldy from Higglesdon Wick comprehensive! My associates are informed by reliable sources that you have long been in possession of documents, a special painting and a famous King 'Henry the Eighth's chair, and you took 'em, and it's time you gave them back now…' (Zarok tried to do 'a Gavin'.)

'A-associates?!' stuttered Master Herbert astounded. Then he recovered himself again, as well as his powers of speech.

'Certainly not boy! Which school do you attend, you young scoundrel?!'

But Zarok didn't answer. He merely espied a box with his laser-like eyes that screamed 'old' to him. He walked calmly to the corner of the room to fetch it, as if something was telling him what to do.

'Leave that deed box where it is!' commanded Master Herbert, practically foaming at the mouth. But Zarok simply passed the old deed box up to the window, where two hands were waiting outstretched to receive it. In a trice, Gavin and Drew poured over the contents…

'Is that the special painting?' demanded Zarok, acting fearlessly. And yes, it was acting. The painting was of a cat –a noble looking tabby that sat by a window with what looked like the school grounds in the background.

'Yes it is a special painting you common rapscallion, but it's of no value to you or anyone else! It is of our old school cat, Brodie!'

This was looking a bit iffy. How could this be Mr Baldwin's painting, if it was of headmaster Herbert's school cat? But Zarok had to simply complete the Hell Dog's mission, on club orders, and trust in the situation. So Zarok moved like a streak of lightning across the room and took the painting from its hook. Then, he calmly passed it up to the outstretched hands of Reubin. Mr Herbert's eyes had by now turned an insane hue of red. Glaring in horror at the space where the painting had resided, he then turned his focus upon Zarok and tried to grab him. Poor Zarok ducked and dived as the portly and furious man chased him in circles around the room, but this gave Zarok the chance to get behind the head's desk.

In the corner, behind his desk, stood a tall backed chair that was enveloped in the black shroud of a headmaster's cloak. Zarok whipped it off, and saw at once it was no less than Henry VIII's chair! As the headmaster threw himself back behind the desk, Zarok skilfully took the chair to the floor and slid it across the room. In one slick movement, he hauled both himself and the chair up, and yet again, it was taken by two outstretched hands belonging to a capable boy called Reubin.

'The outrage! Thief! Stop thief!' wailed Master Herbert, who was now beside himself, while he simultaneously lunged at Zarok in a bid to wring his neck. Zarok, however, simply pushed the portly man back on to his chair and silenced him with a movement of his own. It was utterly spontaneous and breathtakingly exciting to him. He was a young boy, after all, and he didn't consider whether it was right or wrong. But he did it because he knew it was high time for Mr Herbert to shout for the caretaker. Consequently, Zarok braced himself! He pulled back his hoodie and faced the old master head to head with his full-on alien face in plain sight! *Mercy me!*

'You asked me which school I go to Sir! Well, it's a very long way away. In fact, it's beyond planet Mars, and it's also in another galaxy…' Master Herbert opened his mouth to scream, but nothing came out. As protean as a traffic light, his face now turned from red to green. He wheezed a little.

'Good God! My holy aunt!' Master Herbert finally managed in a hoarse, if broken whisper. Now Zarok was beginning to enjoy himself, but he didn't want to get too cocky and mention the Dogs of Hell and so he said: 'My associates have provided me with a nice piece of paper for you to sign. We turn bad deeds into good deeds and try to right wrongs, however far back. We don't want any confession from you; how you acquired Baldy's goods or whatever. All you need to do is sign it! Read it first!' Pale and sweaty and mopping his brow, Master Herbert hesitantly read it. It read thus:

My Dear Mr Baldwin
Many years have passed and we have grown older and mellowed in this wonderful neck of the woods we call Higglesdon Wick. I am man of few words so I hope you will find an apology such as 'sorry' suffices.

It is said with all sincerity from the bottom of my heart. Hereby, I am more than happy to return goods that belong to you and to you only. This includes: a precious painting, a priceless article of furniture from the court of Henry VIII, and a deed box containing irreplaceable documents from Higglesdon Wick. It is a blessed nuisance that these items were purchased from workmen all those years ago, but the past is the past, and I hope the return of your treasures bring you as much delight as they do me in returning them to such an esteemed owner. Congratulations on your generous funding from Lord Cass and I do hope that every single pupil of yours is to be included on your trip itinerary. Please make that plea happen on behalf of me at all costs!

Your good acquaintance
Master Herbert

PS: It was thanks to your wonderful boys, Gavin and Reubin, Lee and Raj, and I believe their friends Drew, Greg and Terry, who begged me to bring your stuff back and make a foolish old man see reason! Truly, you owe the return of your belongings to all of them.

Please go easy on them. I see genius in pupils, and some of the naughtiest can also be the brightest or kindest.

Master Herbert coughed a little. Then he spluttered again and cleared his throat, gasping at the contents of the typed letter in amazement. (Lee had obviously done his homework discovering a deed box too, and writing a decent letter. (Zarok had no idea what had been in that letter and gravitated to the deed box on instinct.) When he had finished, Master Herbert, whose palms were sweating and mouth had gone bone dry (due to the shock of coming face to face with an alien), knew without guesswork what was expected of him. Shakily, he took up a pen and signed his signature in strong handwriting next to the typed words 'Master Herbert'. Then he threw his pen down sulkily, looking desperately up at the window.

'Good! We are done then!' exclaimed Zarok cheerily.

'Thank you very much, Mr Herbert. Thank you kindly!'

'Don't come here again, boy! Don't ask for me again. I have done what you asked of me!' Mr Herbert rasped hoarsely, sweat now pouring from his brow.

'Then we are agreed, if I may ask you…Do not speak of this meeting to anyone!' said Zarok. 'Do not say you have met me yet, as I think that would be for the best. I might just be a relic left from Halloween or I might not…' And with a sprightly leap, Zarok was up and out of the window as nimbly as a bird, before turning back to give the old headmaster a reassuring wave.

As if it was a question of 'yet' thought Master Herbert. No one, *no one,* in this village would believe him if he said he had met an alien, let alone been coerced into giving property back by one! It would have to remain a secret. No question about it! He would have to accept it. He had his position as a headmaster of a private school to think of, as well as his reputation! *Damn that alien and his friends!* But who knows, maybe some good would come of it. The Higglesdon Wick Schools that had separated all those years ago, and his old partner Mr Baldwin, certainly had other grossly mismanaged issues to sort out!

***

By now Gavin, Zarok and Reubin were a quarter of the way up the road, each carrying an item. In their excitement, they had entirely forgotten about the rest of the club waiting for them

'Safe Zarok! I knew the first time I saw you, you was safe!' smiled Reubin.

'Nice one Zarok,' whooped Gav, clapping him on the back and then hi-fiving Reubin.

'Dat shot! But we can't go back for them lot now,' groaned Reubin insensitively. 'This thing is bare heavy!'

'I can't leave my brother, can I?' objected Gavin, pulling out his phone to text him. As he did so, Reubin slapped Zarok on the back for the tenth time. They had already near hugged him to death. Then he remembered Drew hadn't got a phone on him, so he texted Raj. A text came back.

'We w8d 4ages. U dint come so me & Lee went home! Go get Drew tho!'

Gavin texted back: 'Zarok DID it! We got da booty!' He couldn't resist it. He felt bad now that the rest of the club had done the boring look out posting and must have felt completely uninvolved. While Reubin carried on walking home with the painting and Zarok carried the priceless chair, Gavin ran back to get Drew. But as he got close, he felt something was wrong somehow. He was damn right.

Having arrived, he found Drew was there alright, along with Terry n' Greg, but also Gideon, Montgomery and Diggory who had tied their hands to Higglesdon Wick High's school gates with their school ties.

'Leave off of them you eejits! It's getting late now.'

'Enjoy your concert, Gavin?' asked Gideon with a put on laugh. Gavin forced his way past Diggory and begun to untie his recruits knots.

'You're not getting yer ties back for this! Anyway, I'll have to bite them with my teeth to get them off!' came an exasperated Gavin. He didn't need this now.

'You keep 'em! My Dad can afford wardrobes full of ties. We got a better present that we've borrowed from you!' boasted Gideon, picking his cracked lips.

'Oh?'

'Oh yeah! We got Raj's phone! And we just had a lovely text through from Gavin… It says *Zarok did it!* Did Zarok do it Mason? Just who the heck is Zarok?!' Gideon, lip curled, was bristling all over.

'*A who you man?!*' snapped back Reubin, looking ready to spring.

'It's a code name meaning a 'Hell Dog's strength and wit!' replied Gavin with spirit.

'We are going to find out what or who *Zarok is!*' snarled Diggory. Gavin chucked their ties over the gates that were now closed.

'And we see you've stolen a chair from Higglesdon Wick High. There's no way yer goin' to America with a crime like that!' taunted Montgomery.

'*Do yu ting donk!*' came back Reubin with a shrug.

'Bugger off home! You've bugged us enough! Anyway, you wouldn't dare do it?'

Gideon went to kick the chair but Gavin swung it swiftly away.

'Break this and I'll break you!' Was he annoyed!

'We dared to nick Raj's phone though!'

'You've got to give it back or the police will come round your house, you berk!' retorted Gavin lustily as he walked away.

'I've got to scoot now and so has Greg! Sod off, Gideon! Leave us alone!' Terry was fed up of the whole business now.

'Yana! You know it!' emphasised Greg, glaring at Gideon. (A volley of taboo expletives were exchanged...)

'But what if we don't? Hey Terry, you like footie! Say I kick in your Henry VIII chair?' Even Diggory and Montgomery looked worried now. They hated Gideon taking things too far. But Gideon's ego was the size of a balloon and he took a football kick at the priceless chair in Gavin's possession and shouted 'goal!' Greg and Terry and Drew did their best to barricade Gavin.

'Swipe!' yelled Gideon.

'Geroff prat or I'll get my dad on to your dad and he supports Axenwall United!' shouted Terry as menacingly as he could.

'Boot!' yelled Gideon again as if the twilight hours had now turned him into a wolf, or certainly a hooligan. The next time it was Greg who got a kick.

'OW!' He yelled. This was no good, *it had turned real nasty*, thought poor Greg, who was feeling vexed. 'Their popping...' he relayed to Reubin.

'Kick my brother mate and you'll know about it!' Suddenly, a dark hooded figure came running out of nowhere. Fleet of foot, he took hold of Gideon and pulled him down the street before shouting 'Go home!' Then, he went back for Diggory and Montgomery and with an alacritous touch, seemed to move them halfway down the road.

'You go home now too. Now!' yelled Zarok bravely.

'That Zarok, is it?' shouted Gideon shaken, making his way up the street (and fast) with his sidekicks. Gavin whispered something to Zarok, and he ran back after them to seize Raj's phone –end of! Raj would be pleased!

Once in bed and under his comfy duvet with its familiar nautical designs, Gavin said to Drew:

'We gotta take Zarok into school now anyway! We have to try and take you to school Zarok. Going to the concert at the end of the week will be our litmus test. That'll show Gideon and his eejit gang!'

'Yup! Even if he goes for a day or so though Gav,' replied Drew sleepily.

'Well done Zarok! Thanks so much – you did AWESOME! You too Drew, in your own way. Goodnight everyone! See you in the morning...'

But Zarok was fast asleep, and he had the loudest snore in the world!

CHAPTER NINE
THE BOYS TIE UP LOOSE ENDS

Today was the last day of their school term before the children broke up for the Christmas holidays. At around two weeks, the school holidays were not very generous. Nonetheless, Zarok and the Dogs of Hell realised it was unwise to keep the Henry VIII chair, deed box and painting hanging around. They needed to get their booty returned to their own headmaster, so as not to raise too many questions. Not only that, they wanted to get into Mr Baldwin's good books as soon as possible! Then they could start the new term with a clean slate. Therefore, the boys saw fit to get to school early, as this very day was the only time slot left to tie up the ends of this affair.

With that on their minds – despite the excitement of the past evening's events – the boys were up early with their goods. Reubin was already at the bus stop with the precious painting. He was waiting for Drew and Gavin, who arrived five minutes later hauling the deed box and dragging the priceless chair, which had been wrapped in an old binbag. They gave Greg and Terry a five-minute window to turn up, which they did duly; their faces rapt with excitement. It was a crisp and redolent autumn morning. The ochre sunshine burnished the abundance of trees that stretched alongside

Cherry Tree Lane and into Apple Orchard Road, making them russet, chestnut and golden. The bright outlook made the boys feel that fortune was now shining upon them. *Just what would Baldy make of this?*

Gavin, Drew, Terry n' Greg and Reubin all stationed themselves at the rear of the top deck of the bus, taking over the entire back rows. That was OK, it wasn't rush hour yet. Greg sat in the middle at the back, amusing his friends by performing their time-honoured ritual; biting the head off of a green jelly zombie and letting the sticky red fluid trickle down each corner of his mouth. He embellished this act by stretching out to throw his head back, exposing the whites of his eyes, while emitting a disembodied moan. Terry, his all-in-one fan club, cackled in appreciation.

'Give us one, buddy!' begged Terry, his hand halfway into Greg's paper bag.

'Alright, but you owe me one. I've only got six left…'

'Six!' cried the others, now all piling over Greg to practically rip the bag out of his hand.

'Careful they change you like!' warned Greg, gurgling menacingly, whilst animated in a zombie-like stance. Now someone appeared on the top deck and was walking down the aisle as if making towards the rear end, when they stopped in their tracks. It was Alex. He eyed the clan of boys coldly. A couple of them looked familiar.

'I might have guessed it was you and your cronies,' he said, glaring at Gavin.

'Showing us up in the neighbourhood! Well, I'm going to the front, as far away from you as possible, but watch it. I've got eyes in the back of my head!'

'He's alright Alex really' explained Drew to his friends, 'but he suffers from B.S.'

'Poor him… What's that?' enquired Terry, knowing a joke was coming.

'It's Boring Syndrome,' explained Drew poker-faced. This wisecrack went down well with the boys, but alas, moody Alex had heard him.

'It's better than being a pack of complete and utter prats!' he yelled. Then Gavin noticed they were only one stop away from the school!

'OK! Quiet!' he ordered. 'Hey Terry n' Greg, shut up! We gotta sort this fast! Now, I've already thought it would be naff to turn up at Baldy's office with a big grin and the booty.'

'Yeah' seconded Reubin. 'Imagine being at his door with big grins and the booty, s'not right!' The D.O.H. snickered. (Alex got off and stuck his fingers up at them as he turned to descend the staircase.)

'So we won't dump it outside either. Too risky!' added Drew.

'Could you state the obvious, Drew please. I haven't got an idea yet!' said Gavin to an audience of titters before continuing.

'We're gonna do things in a normal way. Take 'em to the reception and ask Mrs Bell if she'll kindly put 'em in Baldy's office.'

'With the note!' added Terry importantly.

'Yes. Well done, Tez! Where is it?'

'It's in the deed box on the top,' informed Drew, serious now.

'Oh! That makes me remember. What happened to the documents that were held at the back of the painting?' asked Reubin to no one in particular.

'Well, you should know. You've been the keeper of it!'

'I think it must have been taken out the back of it by now,' soothed Terry. 'And all the important stuff in the deed box.'

'How should you know?!' snapped Gavin, who secretly imagined he was right. 'Precious little you did last night, hanging on the street corner, texting Greg and doing absolutely nothing!'

'Aw! I was watch out!' protested Terry, quite hurt and reasonably so.

Arriving at their stop, the boys tumbled out of the bus and Lee and Raj were waiting outside the school gates for them, making a show of tapping their watches.

'Hi guys!' greeted Gavin as all the boys gave each other the D.O.H. salute.

Ordinarily they wouldn't have done this if there were hordes of kids milling about, but there weren't. Dragging the painting and the priceless chair across the playground in a bin bag now gashed with holes, the group made their way straight to the reception. Lee and Raj were beaming with admiration at their friends. They were so relieved they hadn't messed this up by oversleeping.

But before they went in, Lee needed to address them.

'We need to clear this up. Me and Raj weren't on the bus with you lot, so the burning question is, do you reckon Gideon's gang suspected Zarok is an alien?! We need to be prepared for that now!' Reubin took the hiatus as a chance to reach into his bag and produce Raj's mobile phone, handing it over to a gleeful recipient.

'No I don't think so. You're right, we need to address this! Raj, you had gone by then. Basically, Zarok was wearing a hoodie, large cool sunnies and gloves, plus it was dark and he acted fast! But Reubin has something to tell you everyone,' warned Gavin, clearing his throat nervously.

'Er…Yeah… Master Herbert knows Zarok is an alien. He pulled off his visor and stuff and also told him that he was from outer space…'

'You morons!' practically shouted Lee. 'O-M-Geeeee!'

'OH NO! Holy moley moley!' babbled Raj, grimacing nervously and hopping on one foot.

'S'alright. It'll be fine!' issued Drew evenly, anxious to move.

'Do wh-haat?!' hollered Terry, with Greg duly echoing him. All the boys usually reacted differently. But this time it was Lee who took it the worst, shaking his head hopelessly. To him and Raj, the show was over.

'You might as well throw your garbage in the bin. It's game over now! I'd get back home and make sure that Zarok's well-hidden Gavin!'

'Yo Lee, level…Ya hear mi bruv?!' reassured Reubin, though sounding less positive now.

'Come on! We dint make an early start for nothing. Let's get on with it! I'm the leader!' rebounded Gavin pompously. So the lot of them trooped into school to the Reception, where this morning Mrs Bell presided. She was surprised to see such a large group of them.

'Good morning boys! You can just come in without knocking you know. I must say it's a surprise to see you all in bright and early!' she exclaimed looking straight at Gavin.

'But you Drew, and Terry and Greg… You aren't supposed to be here, so get to Higglesdon Primary on the double! You've no business here.' While Drew, Greg and Terry got going, Gavin launched straight down to business.

'Uh hum!' he began, majestically clearing his throat.

'Yes?' prompted Mrs Bell.

'We gotta very important letter here for Mr Baldwin from Mr Herbert. Yesterday, he called us in to run a very important errand!' explained Gavin, pleased with himself for thinking of this ruse.

'Why you?' queried Mrs Bell with an expression that read 'unlikely'.

'Why not us!' retorted Reubin robustly. 'We were playing footie and Mr Herbert recognised our school ties. Plus he knows my mum,' lied Reubin.

'What on earth were you doing playing footie outside or in Higglesdon Wick High?' demanded Mrs Bell uncertainly.

'We weren't exactly. We were sort of kneeing the ball,' said Gavin.

'I didn't think you two were that keen on football. You have never made use of our football club' asserted Mrs Bell.

'But Terry n' Greg like it,' replied Gavin with a sickly smile.

Mrs Bell realised this nonsense could go on for a while, so she cut to the chase.

'What may I ask have you bought in…in these binbags?! I'm afraid I will have to look at them boys before I hand them over to Mr Baldwin.'

'Yes. That is fine Mrs Bell,' appeased Lee graciously. Mrs Bell untied the knots and pulled the bin bag aside. She stood contemplating the contents for a few moments before knitting her eyebrows. A faint glint of recognition flickered across her face. Then she smiled and winced, straightening up. Mrs Bell, sporting a sensational red trouser suit, suddenly signalled danger to the boys.

'And you say that Mr Herbert from the High School gave you these items in old bin bags to take to our Headmaster?' She shook her head.

'We shall soon see about that! Of course, I will put these in his office immediately boys, along with the note, plus I shall have to see him myself. But this raises questions. Serious questions! So I am going to chance to ask you myself before this escapade continues. Have you boys stolen property from Higglesdon Wick High?!' demanded Mrs Bell, changing rapidly from harmless to haughty.

'No,' replied Gavin. 'It belonged to our school in the first place!' Lee groaned at this response.

'Right!' said Mrs Bell acidly with a twitch of her nose. 'I will leave the headmaster to deal with you over this. You may go now!' And she turned away with a swish of her scarf.

'Well, that went well!' groaned Raj, head in his hands.

'Don't worry!' soothed Gavin optimistically. 'We know it's above board!'

'She's badass, Mrs Bell' decided Reubin. 'She got sass.'

Terry, Drew and Greg waited outside eagerly to hear how it went, but didn't receive so much as a text. The truth was the boys were now a bit worried and hurried off to the library to start on their overdue homework. That was handy as it was a good forty minutes before class and Lee was on hand to help them. Then Gideon glided over.

'Buzz off!' said Gavin shortly.

'Who was that lad last night, mate? I've not seen him before!' But luckily the librarian came to his assistance.

'Leave them alone while they are trying to work or you may leave!'

***

Mr Anderson's lesson was first that morning, which cheered Gavin up. But he could hardly get too fired up because of the uncertainty of whether he would be included in the USA trip. And Lee was right to worry. They only had Zarok's word that Herbert had said he wouldn't tell. None of the boys could scarcely wait to hear the outcome, but at 11.00am they would do so. Before break, Mrs Bell approached each boy individually to let them know that Mr Baldwin wished to see them promptly in his office at eleven o'clock.

On time, at 11.00am, Gavin, Reubin, Lee and Raj stood in silence outside the Head's office. He swept his eyes over them with a grunt, before opening his office door for them all to file in. His office was brown and constricted and looked as though it was going to collapse under an avalanche of files. The boys felt the room was going to cramp their style. They stood in a line, all hope draining from them as he confronted them, his body framed by a monumental window behind him (which greatly saved the room's proportions.) A personable figure, exuding the air of a Headmaster, he brandished the letter signed by Herbert.

'To save any circuitous enquiries, I am going to telephone Mr Herbert of Higglesdon Wick High in the presence of all of you! He is expecting my call.'

The boys waited with bated breath, their eyes cast down to the floor.

'Good Morning Mr Herbert. Yes, not at all… Really? I've not spoken to them yet. They are here with me! Is that so? Indeed, of course I have read the letter.

From you…I see. Hmm…I have the painting, the deed box and the antique chair. The one inlaid with pearls. That does surprise me Grahame. No, they are not the best students! Indeed, at least we reserve hope for them settling in here at our sought after school. A change of heart?' And so it went on, with the boys hearing one end of the conversation, which became increasingly favourable…

'Not at all! I'm not saying that I don't see their potential. I'm unspeakably fond of them. Yes, they are prone to good deeds… I'm staggered, I must say. You approached them, or they approached you? We must clear that up! You got talking, and they actually broached it. They had read the history of our schools and mentioned the misdemeanour? Innocently playing detective…They were so eloquent that they pricked your conscience…?'

Mr Baldwin viewed Gavin and Reubin suspiciously through narrowed eyes…Eventually, the phone was gently put down.

Mr Baldwin glared at it, sat down weakly and pursed his lips. Then he twiddled his thumbs impatiently, and forgetting the boys for a moment, stared at his returned treasures. Reubin broke the silence.

'It's all alright isn't it Sir?'! he asked, stepping forward to shake the head's hand.

'Safe sir, safe!' he beamed, forgetting himself.

'No, it was not a safe, it was a deed box,' answered Baldy curiously. 'I thought you'd know that Reubin?' The four boys were beaming wildly now, Raj practically dancing on the spot.

'Well I'm blowed!' boomed Mr Baldwin finally. 'I never thought this day would come! Congratulations to all of you! All *is* above board, in fact. You really have done me an outstanding service, and to think you, of all people, got through to Mr Herbert?! He is not exactly known for his benevolence…I need to explain to you that Mr Herbert is not a thief. He and I shared an office many moons ago when the Higglesdon Schools were merged into a primary, a lower secondary school and an upper school. Mr Herbert and myself were both Heads and shared a large office. He was bent on making ours a grammar or Independent school and I was at loggerheads with that, believing in a comprehensive education. The schools split and differentiated in status. There has been some acrimony ever since…'

'But it's all good now Sir. You got your painting of Brodie the cat back,' beamed Gavin, straightening his tie.

'Our beloved school cat!' sighed Mr Baldwin wistfully. 'Now boys, I would like to chat to you about this all day, but it's the last day of term. Now pass me your USA slips!' The boys produced their USA slips with a flourish.

'Excellent!' Mr Baldwin made short work of giving them six merit marks each, a feat unheard of. He added, 'For outstanding altruism' in the comments section. (The boys didn't know what that meant.)

'In short, it means all of you will, without question, be attending the USA trip! As your families will not have to save money for it, and will maybe only need six weeks to arrange the passports, you may be in the first party to go when we come back next term! I believe Mr Anderson is anxious to go early before his wife's due date. So that is settled. There will be no time to disappoint me with any more antics and lateness. Between you and me, this opens a few doors. Mr Herbert and myself will meet over a whisky to plan for competitive sports between our schools and negotiate the return of our snooker table for the sixth form common room. Well done, and off you go!' The boys gave a little cheer!

'Hurray for Mr Baldwin! Thank you Sir!' they said and then scarpered.

'Turn up! He's safe! I'll never call him Baldy again yana!' declared Reubin. But around the corner, Gideon and co. were lying in wait.

'Bet Baldy doesn't know your new friend did all your dirty work, does he? Know what? He soon will, losers! And your new friend is freaky n' all!' But Gavin and his friends ignored them. Once out of the way, they said to each other, 'Crikey! We will have to definitely try to enrol Zarok in the school now!'

CHAPTER TEN

THE DAY OF THE CONCERT ARRIVES

The day of the Monster Metallion's concert had arrived and the boys could barely contain their excitement! True, some of them liked the heavy metal rock band more than the others. Terry, Reubin and Greg liked hip hop, R&B and Garage, and Lee liked techno. However, due to Gavin, Drew's and Raj's enthusiasm, they had been forced into liking them too. The main thing was that they were all going to be allowed to travel to see the band without parents, which was a big deal. However, it appeared that Honour and Raj's dad were going to pick them up after the concert; so there would be no travelling back by a late train. This was all very nice and fair enough, but it posed a problem. How could they avoid the inevitable appearance of Zarok? He was definitely going with them, no question about that! Lee, the brainy one of the bunch, texted Gavin to say: 'He cld travel back on his own by train! Lol! #easy'

Naturally, this was a good proposition, but it somehow seemed like cheating. Gavin and Drew and their mates liked to push the boat out and take a few risks. Rather like a criminal, who after not got getting caught for his crimes, decides to create a scent – a few whiffy tracks for the cops on his tail…

The boys would all be meeting up at Higglesdon Wick train station at six o'clock. The concert started at seven. Gavin's ticket was rumpled but still legible. He spent two hours that afternoon arranging his look and his get up. Gavin and Drew cared little for fashion but today was an exception, as the pair of them messed about with their looks in a bid to emulate their heroes.

'How do I look, Zarok?' asked Gavin who had gelled his hair in taut points across his forehead, and arranged the right and left hemisphere of his hair into tiny horns.

'Er…It's OK, but it is not likely to stay up. You need something stronger to hold it.' Gavin disappeared into Frayre's bedroom and her labyrinth of products.

'I want to look like Ian Firedrake!' said Drew, who had been growing his unruly hair until it was really quite long when the curls were brushed and straightened out.

'Not with a brush and water though! You need hair straighteners and spray!'

Drew tramped up to Frayre's bedroom to spirit away Frayre's straighteners.

'How do you know all this?' Drew asked Zarok, who was watching the procedures perched on the edge of Drew's bed munching a cactus, looking agog.

'I have an eidetic memory' explained Zarok. Sometime afterwards, Drew's hair had been transformed. He found some red spray in Frayre's room, which he'd decided she probably didn't want (as it wasn't with her at college) and used it liberally (until it was empty). It was not quite the finishing touch, however, as he tipped the contents of her shiny blue powder eyeshadow over his locks to boot.

'That's unreal!' shrieked Gavin appreciatively. 'I'm jealous bruv!'

Soon there was the sound of someone shinning up their drainpipe, and a masked face appeared at their window.

'Aargh! Another alien!' laughed Drew remembering that Guy Fawkes night when Zarok had clambered in for the first time.

'Gwaan, Drew, Gav! Hi Zarok! Yeeeaaarrghhh!!!' Reubin screamed, adding sound effects for the benefit of his mask.

'I'm not going in for hair and make-up and all that stuff! No get up! They wear masks too! The Monster Metallions took to wearing masks at the summer festival and you could only tell who was who by their instruments. Whadya think?! I made this myself last night!' Reubin had bought a plain white mask, smeared it with plaster, painted it intricately with coloured patterns, and then added a goatee.

'It looks AWESOME, Reub! You're brilliant at art n' craft!'

But now the friends stopped and noticed that Zarok looked downcast.

'Aw! What's the matter Zarok?' asked Drew kindly. He could guess what was wrong.

'I don't even need to dress up, looking like myself. Like your enemies said, a freak!'

'Yeah but don't you see? It's good to be a freak!' enthused Gavin insensitively.

'Oh come on Gavin. You must see that Zarok feels left out of the equation here!' Reubin started taking a multitude of selfies at this point (insensitively too!)

'Look! That's why it's good. Everyone's gonna be so dolled up in masks and big hair and what-not, that no one will bat an eyelid at him. Safe!'

But Reubin had a better idea. 'Don't worry Zarok, chill! I got another white plastic mask at home. I'll nip back and get it and I'll bring the right paints for it, so you can do your own!' And with that, Reubin was off back down the drainpipe.

'Makes sense that he wears a mask, Gav! And with sunglasses and his hoodie too, no one will recognise he's not human. You wait Zarok! It will be like a zombie party. Noone will look human, so you'll be in the perfect place to get away with being you.'

But somehow, this did not have the right effect. Poor Zarok began to weep. Big fat tears rolled down his translucent face. 'You are right. I can only fit in at a freaks' party!'

But Gavin wasn't in the mood for tears. 'What do you expect?! It's the way it is. You're on our planet! The fact that we like Monster Metallions so much says a lot! They are all individual and wicked! This band are not straightlaced: they dare to be different– and proud! Plus, they can rock the face off the freakin' universe!'

'I am sorry Gavin. I'm really looking to forward to the musical concert, I really am. Especially as I know the music now. I love the drummer!'

'That's the spirit, Zarok! Sort it out!' Reubin was back now with the mask and paints and Zarok soon set to work, working with two paintbrushes at once. His design was so breathtaking, it even outdid Reubin's…

'Drat!' he said meaningfully. 'We will have to swop now! You feel part of things now though, aye Zarok mate?! Make yours a bit worse than mine though, bruv!'

The boys all went off to warm up some pizza and soup, which they made light work of. They were typical lads with gargantuan appetites and could have managed it twice over. Luckily, they planned to get chips on the way! Drew and Gavin's mum would not be back until gone six, and Mrs Beak had arranged the meals on Miriam's instructions. Zarok slid down the drainpipe in case Mrs Beak reported numbers.

'Get back nice and late so we can have an evening's peace for once!' shouted Alex.

'Enjoy yer knitting!' yelled Gavin, and off they all went out of the house, sprinting down the road for the bus to the train station. What freedom! Grown up enough now to attend a rock concert on their own, with not an adult in sight, and holidays from that day on!'

Arriving at the station, Raj could be seen first, clad in a menacing black cloak and some attempt at face tattoos with a black eyeliner crayon. Terry had opted for a glam rock look, trying to replicate the bass guitarist Wolf-eye Virtuoso. In fact, he felt a little sheepish – more sheep than wolf? It was a bit hit and miss. He was wearing a sparkly lilac lurex pullover and a flashy belt borrowed from his uncle. Half of his hair and one eyebrow was dyed green with a concoction from the pound shop.

'That's your mum's top, isn't it?' ragged Greg.

'Yeah it is, and I happen to like it. It looks better on me!' Terry was not averse to defending himself, though he was unsure. He had felt it looked amazing before leaving the house. But soon the station was filled up with a fair number of concert-goers, all with weird and wonderful looks, so the boys felt they blended in brilliantly. In fact, if they hadn't made such an effort they would have looked ridiculous!

Once on the train, the atmosphere was buzzing. Despite all of the white collar commuters, crowds of children had poured in, who mostly had to stand for the duration of the journey.

They struck up *Monster Metallion choruses*, including one that went: *'Thought you were a peach, found out you was a leech… Save me from your creature love…I just can't get enough… Oo-e-ooh! Whoo-e-oo you ou oo!!!'* And also: *'The day of the daemons, I caaame alive! Star struck Venusian we're gonna survive! Dang lang-a-dang-dang…'* (They sang the guitar riffs to boot.)

Mr Anderson and Mr Jackson, who were sitting in the front carriage, turned around. Recognising their pupils, they decided to ignore them.

'I really like 'Andy' so I'm not gonna call him Gulpo anymore,' decided Gavin.

'Zeen. Neither will us,' agreed Reubin. As they were preoccupied with singing for most of the journey, the train soon rolled into Readsford Station. Piling out of the station and taking the short walk downhill to the venue, they discovered throngs of teenagers *en route* all dressed up as members of the band, many in masks and vibrant get-ups! The throng remodelled into a thick queue which the boys joined, noticing they were a long way from the doors, that had not opened yet. The Dogs of Hell, who had never been to an extravaganza of this nature, were not bothered in the least by this detainment; the atmosphere and oneness was electric, as was the craziness of the hordes of ghoulish visages in the half dark.

Interest now turned to Lee's costume. He was wearing a balaclava and a suit that he had squiggled with fluorescent spray, and seemingly chucked some flour over.

'Is that supposed to be Danny Jackal, he wears a white balaclava,' commented Greg, casting a critical eye over the outfit.

'Where am I gonna find a white balaclava, Greg? At least I don't look like an accident at a skip like some people I know,' he growled, feeling silly.

'Don't argue you two, look we're going in!' enthused Drew, joggling Lee. And they surely were! One by one, the boys produced their tickets hoping they would not be ejected due to their age. It was a distinct possibility, and one they had not thought of. They all passed the doorman without incident, until it came to Zarok.

'How old are you sonny?' asked the burly doorman.

'Er… fifteen!' said Zarok hopefully.

'You must be sixteen to come in!' said the doorman scrutinising him.

'Yes, sixteen! I forgot my birthday was last week.'

'When was that?'

'December 12th!' answered Zarok quickly.

'Ticket? OK! Go on in…You look about a hundred!' he said good-humouredly.

'Phew! That was lucky. Well done Zarok,' praised Gavin, slapping him on the back. The boys' hearts had nearly dropped out. It showed that Zarok was going to cut it tonight! Now Drew, Gavin and Zarok surged up the stairs as their tickets had 'circle' printed on them. The other boy's tickets lead them straight into the hall as their tickets indicated 'stalls'.

'Oh NO!' moaned Gavin. 'We don't want to be stuck up here! I wanna be at the front where the action is!' There was nothing for it. Drew and Zarok followed him in word and deed, and so the boys wandered into the hall and down to the end, where they found a secret staircase. They simply scampered down it to meet their friends. It was packed there, and difficult to get to the front.

Minutes later, the lights dimmed and were replaced by a luminous blue phosphorescence, while a soaring, sonic fusion seemed to raise them off the floor. The crowd cheered frenetically! As the Monster Metallions emerged from copious mists of dry ice, the fans went even wilder, but were drowned out by a roaring cacophony that started up. Now the boys could see that mega, golden chainsaws had been set up on various apparatus, and the band was crashing them down upon the metal exhibition with unabashed gusto! Fountains of sparks amidst the thrashing clangour took the boys aback…The tumultuous whirrs became deafening! Greg wanted to look as though his ears could handle it in front of Drew and Gavin, and likewise Raj, whose face was plastered with a strained grin. But Zarok ran towards the exit and soon Drew, Gavin, and the lot of them followed!

Congregating in the hall, with their hands still slapped over their ears while the noise surged through, they mouthed their words to each other…

'Death by noise!' Gavin said, accentuating his chops as he spoke.

'*Ear death by noise!* Sorry to run out but I don't want to go deaf!' said Lee apologetically. They all moved into the garishly carpeted hallway, a bit put out to say the least.

'Aargh! That was splitting me eardrums!' yelled Greg.

'That doesn't sound like the Monster Metallions!' opined Drew simply. The lights were on fully in the hallway, and suddenly Reubin remembered Zarok.

'Don't forget Zarok. We don't want him spotted!' Zarok was busy gazing at a poster advertising the concert, and then took Gavin by the shoulders, reaching up to him.

'We forgot, Gavin. It's a support band first!'

'Well, they can keep their support band! I like metal but I don't wanna hear actual chainsaws all the time! Our ears are bare bleeding!'

The boys relaxed a little, glad that their band had not after all changed their musical style, and went off to the kiosk to buy some ices. For this activity, they all took their masks off. Zarok, soon forgetting himself, joined them. Before long, a familiar sound started up. At last, it was their beloved Monster Metallions! The boys took off back into the arena like bats out of hell. They shoved their way as near to the front as they could go. It was boiling hot and frenzied but they didn't care! Lost in the music they 'shout-sang' along to chorus after chorus. Bastian Basilisk was at his best; playing soaring cadences over a pulsating riot of percussion. When the boy's favourite riffs abounded, they leapt about as best they could, on fire with delight.

Now they had been thrust nearer the front, they could see their heroes at point-blank range! At least, they could see their masks, apart from the rangy lead guitarist who wasn't wearing his. A tumbleweed of flaxen hair flowed carelessly around him, and the boys thought he looked like some kind of demigod from another world. He wore fin-like armour on his arms and his calves were bound with mighty protrusions that grounded his stature. In contrast, the other guitarist looked like a cross between a demonic clown and joker, as he bent over, slapping out a mean, guttural bass.

A seething, sizzling guitar spluttered out before the next track as Danny Jackal yelled out, 'Hullo Readsford! Are you ready to party zombie style?!' The crowd roared with approval. A strutting riff struck out as they sang, *'Zombiefied! Zombiefied! That's how we feel alive a-a-a-alive!'*

And...*'Went to a freaky party– and then you came back... When you survive a ZOMBIE ATTACK!'*

Meanwhile, Zarok had been pushed further back away from his friends. His mask had fallen off in the middle of what was now a manic mosh pit, and he was thrust from side to size within a large body of bods. There was no way he could reach down to get it, let alone find it; it must have been well and truly trampled underfoot! Now poor Zarok felt rather out of his depth in all this ruction. Drew and Gavin were not thinking of him as they were practically salivating, waiting on their last and favourite track, called 'Bosh on Dude.' *'Bosh on in and Bosh it OUT! Bosh on dude right now!'* they yelled.

As anticipated, a lively encore followed after much spirited insistence from the fans. This crowned what had proved to be an utterly spellbinding performance. After lengthy and maniacal applause, the lights finally snapped on to reveal a sweat-sodden audience. It had been two hours of gloriously, contagious ecstasy, and despite everyone looking dishevelled, there was now a sea of bright-eyed, glowing faces! Drew, Gavin, Raj, Lee, Reubin and Terry scanned the stage for any vague sign of their heroes. But the lights were on and it truly looked as if the show was over. Staring at the stage, or around the curtains, was not going to bring the Monster Metallions back. They had after all, shouted, **'Thank you and goodnight Readsford!'** whilst disappearing into an explosion of fire!

The boys found each other fairly quickly and formed a group in the centre of the venue, scarcely being able to drag themselves away.

'That was brilliant!' shouted Gavin, his face shining. 'Bad or what, Reub?'

'It was *awesome* and then some!' raved Drew happily.

'I thought I was going to faint though!' managed Lee.

'Dem was bangin'! Dem was poppin'!' agreed Reubin, quite overcome.

'Yeah, lucky they were chucking water at us and handing out cups of it!' added Greg, feeling grateful for that. 'I mean talk about boiling!' Raj and Terry's make-up had run, leaving their faces bedecked with multicoloured streaks.

The boys contemplated this for a moment while catching a breather.

'Zarok!' shrieked Raj suddenly. The boys checked themselves and then whirled their heads around looking for him. The auditorium was still packed with enthusing fans. There was a steady stream heading towards the main exit, but it was too blocked to get out easily. Then Drew stooped down at the sight of something familiar. It was Zarok's mask...

'OH NO!' They cried in unison. Of course, they had forgotten they were out in public with an **alien** in all the excitement. Gavin stiffened in dismay. Yet Terry was sniggering, finding it funny.

'It's not funny, Tez-face! Come on! We gotta find him NOW!' The boys scoured the floor, and as it thinned out, it was apparent that Zarok was not there! Then, all of a sudden, Reubin spotted him in the Upper Circle.

'There he is! ZAROK man!' he shouted. Certainly, Zarok was there; a lone maskless figure skulking about, clearly visible under a spotlight of all things!

'Oh no!' cried Gavin for the second time. The boys ran for a less packed exit in the corner and fled up the stairs to accost him.

'You should have stayed with us at all times!' he lambasted.

'I couldn't! I was nearly crushed to death!' croaked Zarok.

'Never mind that! Give 'im your mask!' ordered Greg, ripping off Lee's balaclava. But the balaclava didn't do much to hide Zarok's large pellucid eyes.

'Give him your mask, Reubin!' cried Raj. Reubin did not like to take a request from Raj but reluctantly handed it to Zarok. Now two bouncers were approaching them. The Circle was empty but for them.

'Run for it!' shouted Gavin. 'Let's get out of here!' The boys took to their heels and ran out into the foyer and fled down the stairs.

'I would like to see if we can get autographs,' announced Terry, while on the run.

'Yes, we would all like to see them backstage, well…come out the back, but I think we should call it quits, coz you know, Zarok!' explained Reubin exasperated. *As if that wasn't obvious!* he thought.

'At least I caught Von Vamp Scyllla's drumstick!' boasted Terry cheerfully.

'Give us that!' yelled Gavin, trying to tear it off him.

At last, the boys decided they would see if their guardians for the night, Honour and Raj's dad, were there. If so, they would ask them if they could go to the back exit.

'It's not very rock n' roll to do that!' asserted Drew. 'Real rockers would just go and damn the consequences!'

'Really?!' said Gavin, eyebrows raised, and looking at Zarok whose bony hands were exposed (looking positively inhuman.)

'Alright. Let's go!' conceded Drew grumpily. So off the crew went, stomping up the road where many a parent's car was parked. Finally, they saw Honour and Raj's dad waiting for them, waving and calling out.

'So how was the gig?' asked Honour beaming warmly at them.

'Incredible, amazing, absolutely awesome…' they revealed, feeling nervous. This was the moment they dreaded. Raj still looked enraptured.

'*Irie!* Now, there's eight of you. Lee and Raj are going in Raj's dad's car…' Raj's dad opened the car door for the boys to jump in, but they didn't.

'And I expected to take five of you, which I don't know if I can do as it is! It will be a squeeze. Who is that?! There certainly isn't room for six!' asserted Honour. 'Lord have mercy!' The boys went quiet.

'Who is that?' asked Honour again, this time in a low voice to Reubin, taking him aside.

'He's a friend of ours,' answered Reubin plainly. In Higglesdon Wick, just about everyone knew everybody, so all of their friends and acquaintances were known to parents.

'What is your name then?' Honour asked Zarok. There was an awkward silence. Reubin raised his eyes up to the sky.

'OK, where does he live? Does he live near us?' enquired Honour more gravely.

'Higglesdon Wick,' answered Terry breezily.

'Well, I can take him if he lives near Lee and my family!' offered Raj's dad.

'Y-eees. Thank you Azis, but we need to know who he is first! If you don't want to tell me perhaps Drew can!' said Honour looking a trifle put out now.

'If he's your friend, who is he?' Another strained silence. Then…

'Hmm… The concert is over now, so if you can remove your mask, I can see who we are taking home! If it's just anyone, it wouldn't be OK boys!' explained Honour, now assuming the demeanour of a village policeman.

'Plus we need to know *where* we are taking you!' insisted Honour, now putting her hand out to pull at Zarok's mask. The boys gasped in horror.

'No! Don't!' squeaked Zarok, and in a thrice he turned and fled. Just turned on his heels and run for it…Gone?!!

'Well I never! What a strange friend you have. Who is he?!' demanded Honour, her glittering eyes gracing her now taut features.

'Er?' said Gavin a bit dumbfounded.

'We will have to run around to find him now or it will be dangerous for him! Honestly. We came to pick you up, not embark on some fiasco, Reubin! I don't mind, but poor Raj's dad!'

'He's O.T. now yana,' mumbled Reubin, pinching Gavin.

'I will stay and search with you, Honour,' he said pleasantly, but looking vexed.

'It doesn't matter!' blurted out Gavin. 'Really, we just met him at the concert, but we got on so well he feels like one of us!'

'Well, you don't know him then! And it's best you don't offer a lift to strangers without clearing it with me first. Frankly, he is rather rude – or not a passenger I would take if he can't speak for himself! How odd!'

Honour, who was looking rather glamorous in a red dress and her top-notch bling, threw Gavin and Reubin a sceptical glare, and then the party got going. The incident rather took the gloss off of what had been an awe-inspiring night. Furthermore, in the boy's minds, they were thinking the same and inwardly terrified, especially Gavin. *What was going to happen to Zarok now, with him so far from home?!* Reubin, Terry and Greg normalised things in the car on the way back by chatting about details of the concert, but Gavin and Drew were too beside themselves. The boys said their goodbyes amidst whispering and knowing looks, and Gavin and Drew couldn't get in fast enough. They hardly greeted their parents before going straight to their room to plot.

'Goodnight mum and dad, we're finished!' explained Drew.

'Now what?' raved Gavin.

'Dunno!' said Drew miserably, diving under the covers.

'We might never see Zarok again!' wailed Gavin, gazing out of the window bleakly.

'But what would he do? He'd get on the train the way we came and come back home!' reasoned Drew.

'That's just it! Get on a train that is neon lit... The train inspector gets on and...?!'

'And he shows his ticket with his head down,' said Drew hopefully.

'Yeah, knowing him, he'll go exploring or something!' Poor Gavin was in bits.

They waited up for Zarok and their impatience was eventually rewarded. Finally, there was a knock on the window and, yes, it *was* Zarok!

'Zarok! Thank goodness! What happened?' belted out Gavin, throwing up the sash.

'I just came home on the train' answered Zarok simply. And that was the end of it, or so they thought, until the following evening.

The family were together, Gavin and Drew, Billie, Alex and their parents. They were sat in the front room with the television on watching the news.

'Oh, this is good, Gavin!' said his mum. 'There's going to be coverage of your concert!' The boys sat up with interest. The footage showed hordes of youngsters dressed to the nines, homing in on the scarily masked faces. The commentator came on reporting:

'The gory sets and pyrotechnic wizardry made for an eye-popping show last night when the Monster Metallions

played the next leg of their tour. Parents were advised to stay at home as something like a scene from 'Thriller' descended upon Readsford. The concert went well and was managed safely without incident. However, many witnesses are asking whether the fans of this highly individual act, which some declare to be 'a band of lunatics', have gone too far by vamping up their dress as if it were Halloween, or even radically altering their facial appearances!'

Now the lyrics of 'When you survive a Zombie attack!' could be heard being chanted by the crowds, and a scene to rival any headline act at a sports stadium followed. Well, that's what the boys considered it to be. Cameras rolled over the sea of fans, masked or made up to the nines. Drew and Gavin were glued to the screen, avidly looking for themselves. Close-ups appeared of a scary white clown, and a man with horrific looking facial piercings. And then, horror of horrors, the boys' faces collapsed at what they saw. Gavin sat forward and Drew fell back on the sofa…

'I say, that one looks extremely freakish!' exclaimed Miriam, looking aghast at a spotlit face that was clearly a bare-faced Zarok! The boys gasped out loud in astonishment as the camera zoomed in on him and stayed there…

'What the craic! That kid looks like he's undergone some gruesome face modification! What lengths people will go to for fashion. He looks shocking! And caked!' reproved Brian, looking disgusted. 'Are those contact lenses or are his eye whites dyed black? Good grief!'

'It is a shame, his poor parents! I blame them!' rejoined Miriam. The boys said nothing but grabbed hold of each other to steady themselves. *Damn! Zarok was on TV!*

'So eerie… I'm sorry Drew. I don't approve of some of those fans. They look evil! And talking of eerie; God only knows what it reminds me of, but I'm feeling eerie in my own home lately. It always feels like there is someone else here! It's like we are being watched. *Tis quare to be sure…*' Brian turned his gaze on the now unflinching boys. (It was a mechanism that they had perfected with the Dogs of Hell, to deflect arising trouble.)

'Have you had anyone here?' enquired Brian bluntly, 'because I doubt we have ghosts…' Gavin found it quite hard to lie to his dad.

'Um…Uh huh! Well, we have had Terry staying round quite a bit. He wasn't getting on at home,' offered Gavin lamely.

'But Terry comes from a very nice family. I know he regularly goes to see the football with his dad! And why wouldn't you ask us first?!'

'They didn't want to,' tried Billie helpfully.

'I mean Greg!' tried Gavin (even more lamely).

'You won't get any sense out of those two. Just look at them! They're a couple of sandwiches short of a picnic,' announced Alex, carefully selecting a favourite expression of their father's. He'd been quiet up until then, watching the Monster Metallion's footage with open disdain. 'Imagine liking that tacky band? They would!' But he added, 'To be honest mum, I don't think they've had anyone there. They make as much noise with just one of them on their own!'

'Mmmm…What about my cacti, missing sweet potatoes and more. I'm fed up of it! *Quare it is to be sure.*'

'Well, there's only one way to find out!' decided Brian rather grimly.

'I'm going to take a look!' and with that, he left the room to make his way to the boys' bedroom. But the boys had planned for this eventuality and started whistling. Moments later, Brian burst open Gavin and Drew's door, and tore the covers off the bed. No one was there! Smart Zarok had made it to the garden shed in record speed, albeit leaving the window wide open. Yet there was one other clue. A cactus stood in plain sight in the middle of a carpet with a munch taken out of it... It was returned to a mystified Miriam.

'You could try talking them into behaving themselves but it's biscuits to bear! They get a gas out of doing a number on people!' concluded Brian tersely.

Later that evening, Miriam told the children they would all be going up to Frayre's college to see her play, 'The Silver Sword', by Ian Serallier.

'I won't be going. I'll stay back as I can't fit in the car,' voiced Alex moodily. This posed a real problem. *Alex left in the house alone, with Zarok there?!*

'Please go Alex! You'll really miss out. I already know it will be so good. Also, Frayre won't be happy if you miss it,' pleaded Drew kindly.

'Please go Alex,' echoed Billie imploringly.

'That settles it!' said Brian. 'We will make a relaxing trip of it and all go by train. You too Alex! Get away from that computer for once! We will get a nice takeaway, and that will be a good start to the holidays for you.' Gavin and Drew couldn't believe their luck. So many near misses and yet Zarok's luck and theirs had not run out yet. But it was all getting rather stressful!

***

CHAPTER ELEVEN
ZAROK ATTENDS HIGGLESDON WICK COMPREHENSIVE

Frayre's school, The Young Bard's Academy of Performing Arts, had pulled off a first-class season. All of their shows had been performed in front of a full house for once. Frayre's year group's play, 'The Silver Sword', was no exception and had been declared an unqualified success! Gavin and Drew had been swept away by the performance, and even Alex (torn away from his machines) enjoyed himself. When the show was over there was not a dry eye in the house, and it signalled the end of Frayre's term. While the Masons enjoyed their ices, she helped backstage before joining her family. (By that time, the boys had already forgotten it and had their heads together, plotting about Zarok.) With a bulky rucksack on her back, Frayre ran to greet her mum and dad in the foyer, then dumped her stuff under the table, leaning back as far as possible on her plush velvet chair. She had put her all into the show and was knackered, yet still on a high.

'Aren't you going to say how brill my show was?!' she demanded of Gavin, smiling with her eyes closed.

'Oh yes! We loved it, didn't we Drew? You was brilliant in it, but it seems ages ago now!' Gavin replied. Frayre screwed up one eyelid at her brother.

'I liked the bit when you took your bows,' offered Drew. 'It would've been cool to have you come down straight afterwards, still in your costume!' Frayre was glad to be coming home for the Christmas holidays, travelling back with them, chatting away while the evening train rattled along. It continued to be a merry evening.

But all that was a while ago now and the Christmas holidays had passed fairly uneventfully since then. The Masons had descended on Grandma for Christmas, which had been a fairly gay, if not rowdy occasion with constant telling offs (in case they gave their grandmother a heart attack.) The presents had been passable, but nothing to write home about. There was the usual plethora of socks and stationary, chocolates and shampoo. The truth was it proved hard for the parents to manage too much extravagance, what with looking after all of them. Billie was the happiest, having received a brand new scooter and an adorable doll that could be packed into a white leather case, which had pockets for a comb and hairbrush.

There then followed a visit to Drew and Gavin's uncle, which was less than festive. Drew declared him 'a boring old f**t' and Gavin was sick and tired of him after only half a day. Frayre pampered herself at home when she got back and played lots of 'had' with the children around the house and garden. The New Year went off with a bang! Neighbours and friends provided merriment, popping in until many of them piled on to Cherry Tree Lane to watch the fireworks, see the New Year in and 'first foot' with coal, money and cookies. There were various community parties to attend after that, with celebrations of traditional music, dancing and culture, which were proving popular that season. Higglesdon Wick was good like that.

Poor Zarok had missed out on just about all of this. Realising this, Gavin had thoughtfully brought his (repacked) Christmas sock back home for Zarok to open. It had been hard for the boys to relax over the spells away, what with Zarok back at home! But they shouldn't have worried since he was alone. *Yet they wondered what mischief he'd get up to, if any.* However, it seemed that Zarok had been on his best behaviour, not wanting to spoil the boy's Christmas. Drew had left him a sack of sweet potatoes, two jars of molasses, castor oil, and three cacti…It had meant that Drew's Christmas presents had been stingy and bought from the pound shop. Biscuits had been addressed to 'both mum and dad'. Gavin and Alex had got nothing. He'd bought his grannie a bar of value soap… His uncle got a pencil…Yes, it was expensive keeping Zarok! Meanwhile, Zarok had kept up his appetite for amusement by making friends with the dog, Roji.

Therefore, that evening, which happened to be the one before school started again, the boys decided to reward Zarok by endeavouring to give him some kind of life by risking taking him to school with them! The boys were holed up in their bedroom ploughing through Drew's old clothes to try and put together a uniform for him. Then, Gavin remembered he'd hardly done any homework, so he pulled open an exercise book to try and multi-task. *Phew,* it seemed there was a lot of preparation to do for the next day.

'Give th' Dogs o' Hell a bell or text for a pre-school meeting!' ordered Gavin, while frantically scribbling in his science notes. Drew had used the monotonous time at his uncle's to sort out his homework. Mind you, it wasn't as demanding as Gavin's.

'I'm afraid to go in, Drew! I don't want to let you down!' lamented Zarok, visibly distraught. He was now kitted up in a dirty white shirt and school tie.

'You won't let me down, Zarok. You're going to Gavin's school!'

Gavin grinned, not looking up. He pulled out a history book now and started swotting up.

'OK dude! Very funny. I know you are trying to help me, but I really did enjoy staying in your home, you know! You don't have to think I was sad and fed up!'

'You were 'fed up' alright! You ate all them sweet potatoes!' quipped Drew. Zarok was viewing himself in the mirror, and went all the way back towards the window to get a fuller view.

'Goodnight boys!' called Miriam up the stairs. 'Get to bed now! Sleep well!'

'Goodnight!' shouted Zarok with them spontaneously, then immediately slapped a hand over his mouth in shock!'

'You blithering eejit!' rasped Drew. 'Lucky we shouted night too…' As if to stamp out the indiscretion, Zarok switched the main light off.

'Don't!' yelled Gavin. 'I gotta finish this!'

'So…Shall I wear my sunglasses tomorrow? And should I wear my hoodie up?!' whispered Zarok to Drew, as he turned around to face him.

Drew sat up on his bed to examine his alien friend.

'You look good Zarok…Yes! You must wear your sunglasses and hoodie at all times, and I can dig out some gloves for you too.' Drew was secretly glad that Zarok was going in with Gavin and not him.

But Gavin, as if reading his thoughts, looked up from his geography homework and said: 'I might need you to sneak into my school for this. I been thinkin' about it. You do a blindin' impression of Baldy.'

Drew was happy to leave the details until the meeting. He sat down to play a round of cards with Zarok, which they played silently, nervously… The next day was going to be very, risky, and it could spell the end for their time with Zarok. They didn't want to argue with Gavin though. Plus, it seemed they needed to move the situation on somehow. It just seemed right, didn't it? The next morning, Miriam had laid the table for breakfast but had already left for work and taken Billie with her. Cereals were free standing on a crisp blue tablecloth, and there was a large jug of creamy milk. Fruity smoothies were poured out for them, plus some rashers of bacon, croissants and leftover boiled eggs that had sadly gone hard and cold. The boys tucked in heartily, enjoying it. They needed their strength up for the day ahead! Zarok emerged out of the kitchen in his school uniform having come down the back stairs. Roji leapt up at him, barking joyfully. Zarok was beaming from ear to ear.

'Cripes! Are we really doing this?' gulped Drew, almost choking on his bacon croissant.

'Come on, bruv! Come on, Zarok! We're going to be late!' yelled Gavin by way of an answer. Bedecked in crumbs and a milky white moustache, Gavin hauled up his schoolbag from a kitchen chair and made for the door, pulling the keys out of his pocket. Zarok and Drew did the same and made off after him. Outside, Reubin was waiting, glowering.

'Mate! I rang for you twice! Come on! The meeting! *Oh zeen!* Zarok! You really are bringing him!' added Reubin, looking gobsmacked as Zarok shyly emerged. Reubin looked him over unable to hide his astounded reaction. But not wanting to offend Zarok, he simply said: 'Come on! Let's run!' So without ado, the boys ran down the road. They would not stop, except for the bus. At least if they ran, they were always on the move, getting somewhere.

'Ha ha! In fact, we've beaten the bus!' managed an out of breath Terry, who had run after them and caught up eventually. His faithful sidekick Greg was with him, tactlessly and openly giggling at Zarok, whilst making a pathetic attempt to cover his mouth.

'Cycle sheds!' ordered Gavin glaring at him. They all trooped into Gavin's school, knowing that dutiful Lee and Raj would be waiting for them. They were never, ever late! The boys were really glad to see each other as they had been truly too busy in the holidays to keep up with each other properly. They'd had to see their folks at different times, which had been a pain! So this time the Dogs of Hell did not act out their usual military style salutations and what not, but fell upon each other in a group hug, slapping each other on the back like mad.

'I'm so glad to see you, but not so late!' scolded Lee. 'If you really are taking him in, we have only got twenty minutes to plan it now!'

'So who's taking the meeting, me or you?!' contested Gavin. Terry and Greg were looking unusually spanking clean in their freshly washed and pressed uniforms, their faces looking scrubbed.

'He does *look* like an alien…' started Raj carefully, throwing Zarok an apologetic glance. The boys, who were all stood in a circle, now made themselves more comfortable by propping themselves up on various bicycle seats or the stands that held them.

'OUT of bounds!' shouted Reubin at a small lad trying to leave his bike.

Terry solicitously took out his 'Danger KEEP OUT' sign and attached it in front of the entrance. The cycle sheds were not on open display, but situated around a narrow corner, so only one cyclist at a time could get in, wheeling their bike. But that would not be happening now…

'Twelve minutes left!' sighed Lee exasperatedly, his eyes poised on his phone.

'OK! Let's get on with it!' announced Gavin, his eye meeting the gaze of all his favoured members.

'As you can see…We've got Zarok with us!'

'Hi!' said Zarok giving them all a little nervous wave.

'Now! He's gonna wear his sunglasses and hoodie all day,' started Gavin.

'Yeah, like Baldy's gonna let him do that!' challenged Terry sniggering.

'What is he going to do when we've got P.E.?!' asked Raj trying to get practical.

'He won't be doing P.E.!' stated Gavin simply.

'Now this is what I wanna ask you, especially Lee. Zarok's going to have a rare disease, which means he can't take off his glasses or take down his hoodie! BUT…What could that be?!' Gavin looked pointedly at Lee while they all racked their brains. But Reubin got there first.

'There was a pop star, it might have been Jackson, and he couldn't go into the light! He had to wear shades and go round with an umbrella!'

'OK! We will go with that then. What's the condition called?'

But no one knew and there was scant time to research it on the internet.

'There is a skin condition called impetigo,' revealed Lee. 'You can also have psoriasis!' The others looked impressed at this.

'How do you say it though!' prompted Drew. Lee said it and they all tried to pronounce it. He shook his head wearily.

'More to the point,' went on the savvy Lee, 'how do you think you can just march Zarok in? You have to enrol. His parents would have to be dealing with it all. Why didn't you think of that? You should have phoned me last night!'

'What's *henrol*?' asked Drew innocently.

'OMG! Even I know that!' said Greg.

'Think of something dups!' urged Reubin frantically. 'Time's running out!' Poor Zarok looked totally freaked out now, pulling at his tie for comfort and feeling totally out of his depth. *If only he could stay right here!*

'Er…Well, thanks everyone for your help! I vote, me n' Reubin, Lee and Greg come in with me to the office…'

'Why not Raj, Terry and Drew too,' put in Lee sarcastically. Gavin ignored him.

'Lee will gloss over any mistakes we make, and we'll say he's got that skin disease –pso…r pso-r-piss –or whatever it's called. Oi Drew…You'll have to be late for school! Drew will hide in the loos and then sneak along to Baldy's office, and phone in pretending to be his mum the minute we text him.' Now Terry cracked up laughing, leaning on Reubin for support.

'Not his mum! Mr Baldwin himself!' scolded Lee. 'He can do it!'

'Oh yeah, I forgot! Well, it's all sorted then! Wish us luck everyone and let's go!' The boys all piled their hands together, shaking them vigorously, before making an action as if letting off a tumbler of confetti.

'Good luck Zarok! Good luck!' they all hailed with feeling. Then the boys parted.

Gavin, Reubin and Lee, and of course Zarok, made their way to the secretary's office. They decided to let Greg get back to his school, as he'd only be coming along for moral support. Before they got to the office, Gavin straightened his tie and whispered...

'Don't forget, hood up Zarok!' and smiled at his friend reassuringly. *Perhaps it would all work out brilliantly!* Already Gavin had got a text: 'lol...Remember he's an alien. Be careful!!!'

It was from Raj. Poor Raj could get very emotional and being a sensitive soul, he was quaking in his boots for them. He was also aware of the amount of trouble this action could bring on them. He thought that the boys were too familiar with Zarok now to see it. But Gavin's throat was dry, Reubin's stomach was in knots and Lee was bracing himself for every face-saving tactic.

'Good morning Mrs Bell!' he announced, overdoing it.

'Good morning Gavin,' answered Mrs Bell curtly without looking at him, her eyes fixed only on Zarok (and rather critically too.)

'Who's he?!' she demanded bluntly, tapping her red spectacles and blinking.

'Oh him, he just, er... I say, did you have a nice Christmas, Mrs Bell?'

'Yes, Gavin. And why, may I ask, have you bought this boy along? Did you find him under the Christmas tree?' she asked rather unkindly. Fortunately, Mrs Bell was a tad short-sighted. That did not, however, prevent her from being a stickler for the rules. She took a breath to speak but Lee got in first.

'Mrs Bell. We found this boy outside the school gates this morning. The poor thing was lost. His name is Zarok!' Mrs Bell stared at Lee before sweeping round to talk to her secretarial assistant, Miss Speakwell. After a quick conversation and a scanning of the lists she turned to the boys with a glint in her eye.

'He is not on any of our admission lists. He cannot just turn up and decide he wants to come!' she declared, now busying herself with a pile of paperwork, expecting them to just leave.

'Er…Mrs Bell?'

'Yes Gavin. Have I not made myself clear? I'm sorry Zarok, but you've not enrolled have you?' said Mrs Bell, looking squarely and formidably at Zarok, who was trembling from head to foot.

'B…but we found him in the playground…on his own! He said his mum had come in, in the holidays and…'

'We're not in during the Christmas holidays. We break up then! Good grief!' cried Mrs Bell, who appeared as a terrifying vision to the boys this morning, in a loud orange pullover, crowded with multicoloured pendants. Miss Speakwell was trying not to laugh.

'We found him in the playground and he said, *not us*, that his mum contacted the school, and it was all sorted that he could attend! She couldn't escort him as she's gotta go to work this morning!' insisted Reubin, bravely upping the ante.

'I would like to attend school this morning!' stated Zarok, feeling he must do his bit to try and persuade her.

'Would you indeed?!' replied Mrs Bell with a note of rage in her voice, which was unlike her. Perhaps she was not yet ready to be back at school.

'Then, why are you wearing a hoodie pulled up and sunglasses then! Looking like a right hooligan, I might add. I am sure you know that it's not an acceptable dress code for any school!' Mrs Bell shot up from her seat to see to a couple of other children and check some wall charts. When she turned round, it was in disbelief, as the boys had stayed put.

'Come now boys! Are you still here? I'm sorry Zarok! You can't come to school here. I am the head secretary and most admissions go through me! Now get to class, boys! The bell went five minutes ago.' But Gavin who was stubborn and would never give in, had already motioned to Reubin (who had niftily shot out a text to Drew hiding in the loo.) It was to tell him to be on standby. Then, Reubin acted as though to obey Mrs Bell.

'Alright Miss. Have a good day. I'm going to science now.'

In reality, Reubin zipped over to Mr Baldwin's office instead. Looking through the glass window, he could see it was empty! There was no time to lose! Drew was already hanging around the toilet door and pegged it along to the Head's office, as Reubin was frantically beckoning him over. He threw himself into the office and at the phone. Meanwhile, Reubin stood blatantly on watch outside, ready to send any teacher packing if needs be, including Baldy himself.

Gavin was still making his presence felt in the secretary's office.

'If you think his appearance is funny miss, it's because he's ill, aren't you, Zarok? He's got that skin condition, called psro-p-sor- psiss. So he's got to wear a hoodie to keep him out of the sun. And he's got…the same illness a pop star had; who had to go around with an umbrella and sunglasses, as you know… he's sensitive to…'

'GAVIN!' bellowed Mrs Bell. 'That really is enough! You seem to know an awful lot about this boy who you only just met in the playground! Now even Reubin has gone off to class, and if you won't desist from this nonsense right now…I'll…'

The phone suddenly rang out and Mrs Bell grabbed the receiver looking harassed, while tidying her hair with one hand, as if to compose herself.

'Yes Mr Baldwin. Yes indeed… Is that so? Well, I've had Gavin in the office with me who found him and brought him in…Of course… If the L.E.A. state he must take a school place here as a matter of urgency…We can temporarily enrol him. Yes, I'll see to it. No! It's no problem at all Mr Baldwin. Will do immediately!' Mrs Bell put the phone down and looked at Zarok again, at a loss. Finally, she sighed and said quietly and resignedly, 'OK boys. It looks as though Zarok is going to be able to come and join us in our school today. He can go to class with you, Gavin, for now.' *Result!*

'Can you leave me your phone number, Zarok?' asked Mrs Bell shrilly.

'I'm afraid I have lost my phone,' replied Zarok as sorrowfully as he could.

'I wonder that I couldn't have guessed that,' muttered Mrs Bell dialling out.

'NOW GET TO CLASS BOYS! Welcome to Higglesdon Wick Zarok and enjoy your day!' And finally the boys left, whooping in the corridor and doing victory salutes as Drew and Reubin joined them.

Drew had done an excellent job of pretending to be Mr Baldwin. He had perfected the accent by talking into a handkerchief. And being the naturally talented mimic that he was, meant that he had pulled it off. It was too good to be true!

Having done his good work, Drew didn't want to wait around now. He took to his heels and sped off to his school next door. He was going to be really late, but he doubted if it mattered on the first day back.

'Will it be 'too good to be true' when Mrs Bell relays that to Mr Baldwin?' asked Lee.

'Oh no! I didn't think of that. Don't spoil things, Lee! We can keep it going somehow. When, or rather *if*, things go wrong, we will have to pull him out, but I bet it's alright now. I mean he's allowed here today, so why not tomorrow?!' Gavin felt frothy with idealistic optimism after what they had just achieved. Lee shook his head groaning, but said no more.

While Drew was getting a dressing down, having bumped slam bang into Miss Jacobs on the way in, Gavin was racing up to his science lesson, with Reubin, Zarok and Lee in tow. Their science teacher, Mr Bunsen, was a sort that didn't mind the odd, noisy intrusion as they burst through the door. Mr Bunsen (who was a rather doddery old chap) was blessed with an outstanding teacherly feature – an optimism, which saw potential budding genii in all of his pupils. Therefore, he took an untimely intrusion as a sign of overt enthusiasm. It was a nice classroom, if rather old fashioned, with rows of long wooden worktops throughout.

'Good morning Mr Bunsen,' shouted the boys as they rolled in, taking their pews on high stools at the back of the class.

'Sorry we're late Sir!' said Lee.

'That's quite alright boys. I've no doubt you were swotting up on your science before the lesson in the library. I've been around long enough to know all your tricks,' he expounded with a rickety-toothed grin. 'Now where were we?'

'We were talking about space,' volunteered Diggory, who was now boring his eyes into Zarok as he pulled out his mobile. In fact, he wasn't the only one.

'Yes, indeed. Let's continue with our questions!' rallied Mr Bunsen.

'1927 was a key date in scientific discovery when *who* discovered that the universe is continually expanding?'

'Marie Curie!' called out Sian.

'I'm afraid not, Sian. Good try. Gavin, can you tell us?'

'George Lemaitre!' answered Gavin once Lee had whispered the answer to him.

'What did Hubble show in 1929?'

'Hubble showed that the galaxies were moving away from each other. This forms the basis of the Big Bang Theory,' explained Geeta hurriedly.

'Class! I knew that,' groaned Reubin. 'Can we put our hands up, Sir?!'

Zarok was slumped over his part of the worktop, head down. He pursed his lips knowing he mustn't say anything. Zarok was excellent at science. However, where he came from, his race didn't believe in the Big Bang Theory. But if he explained the hypothesis that he thought was superior, it would draw attention to himself.

'New boy at the back… What did Einstein publish in 1919?' Poor Zarok was dumbfounded. He'd never heard of Einstein. A show of hands reaching up to the ceiling accompanied by strains of 'me, me, me!' erupted…

'Imagine not knowing that!' sneered Gideon, 'I tell ya, that kid's a freak show!'

'Raj! Can you tell us?' Raj was glad to come to the rescue.

'In 1919, Einstein published his paper on General Relativity! Zarok knows it Sir, but he's a bit shy…'

'ZAROK?!' squealed Gideon, as his sidekicks – Josh, Montgomery and Diggory fell about – creased up with mean laughter. Soon, the whole class were joining in. The girls who were often much kinder, and interested in the new boy, were now openly turning around in their chairs tittering. Verity and Sian, who had a tendency to be catty, were giggling hysterically.

'Oh no! We need a normal, new name for him, like Arun or something!'

Reubin whispered to his shamefaced friends. *It was too late now!*

'Hey! Where d'ya come from Zarok? Do you come from out there in the universe?!' cajoled Diggory.

'Order please!' begged Mr Bunsen almost apologetically.

'Ahem. New boy, I believe Zarok is your name. Now there is nothing wrong with unusual names. In my university days, I had a colleague who named his son Copernicus in honour of his hero. He named his daughter 'Eternal!' However, we usually ask our students to stick to a school uniform code, pointless as it is. Would you be able to remove your hooded garment, Zarok?'

'No, he wouldn't!' shouted Reubin hotly. 'He hasn't got a blazer yet!'

'Ah, diddums! Can't afford a blazer!' yelled Montgomery, pretending to play an air violin. *This class was turning into anarchy, Mr Bunsen sighed to himself. Yet, if only this new boy was really from out of space…What a fascinating science lesson this could be!*

'Mr Bunsen! The new boy has got a rare skin disease; he's light sensitive. Sadly, he must be covered up hence the sunglasses and hoodie,' explained Lee diplomatically. The girls ummed and ahhed now. Mr Bunsen pricked up his ears.

'That is interesting. Pray, what is it called?'

'It's called chronic acne!' yelled Gideon nastily.

'But if he has his eyes covered up he must be suffering from photophobia!' guessed Mr Bunsen, who was now gazing long and quizzically at Zarok. What an odd appearance he had…

'Yes that too!' agreed Gavin, standing up quickly to make a point.

'So let's put an end to any stupid, cruel and rude wisecracks. May we know a little about you, Zarok? We may get to know you better, and you us, in the next lesson, of course…'

'Yeeess. Thankyou Mr Bunsen.' But Zarok's soft American lilt was drowned out by the school bell. 'Brrrrrrrrriiiiiiiinnnnngggg!'

'Saved by the bell!' realised Gavin, raking his hands through his hair, and addressing *'whew!'* to an open window. Then he gathered his bag up, his friends quickly following suit, and headed for the door as fast as possible. But the other kids, nearer the exit, had got there first, and a bunch of girls and boys were waiting for Zarok.

'Hello Zarok! Is that really your name?' asked Ife with a big smile.

'No, it's zitty, Zargoid! Innit Za-wreck?!' sniped Gideon, going for his sunglasses. But Gavin, Lee, Raj and Reubin packed around Zarok tight, like bodyguards. Typically, Gideon's gang of Josh, Diggory and Montgomery were trying to prise them apart.

'Fight! Fight!' screamed Verity.

'Leave sunglasses boy alone!' yelped Melissa and her friend Jocelyn.

'BALDY!' yelled Reubin…Suddenly, the throng split, pegging it to the end of the corridor and then out of the door into the playground. Halfway there, Gavin and his friends turned and fled in the opposite direction; where, of course, no Mr Baldwin was visible. He was too partial to his breaktime tea and biscuits to be patrolling the corridors then.

Soon, the boys had made it to the back of the library to catch breath and reflect on the morning events.

'You alright now, Zarok?' asked Reubin, crunching into an apple.

Gavin sat in a corner relaxing with his legs out and an open snack box propped on top. Out of this he pulled a mini cactus for Zarok and a fudge biscuit for himself.

'Well, I think that went as well as could be expected! They don't know he's an alien!' said Gavin, a detectable note of triumph in this voice.

'Yet…' said Lee, who felt it to be doomed if he was honest. The more excitable Raj said: 'Are we going to take him to P.E. next then? That should be fun!'

'It would be fun Raj…It should be, if those blasted bullies, Gideon's gang, weren't around!' This gave Reubin a thought as he slouched against the wall.

'Let's just lock 'em up for the afternoon! I'm sick of em! *Wastemen!*'

'And they are a liability!' proposed Lee, looking grave.

'Come on then!' rallied Gavin, happily looking for serendipity.

Soon Gavin and his friends came upon that serendipity in the shape of a cupboard near the end of the corridor, where they had left Gideon's mob after the science lesson. Luckily, it was open. It held stuff like brooms, buckets and mops.

The boys went inside there but left Zarok outside. Then they sent Reubin out to wait outside, near to the cupboard. They found what was bound to be a spare key, nailed up on the wall. The boys knew that Gideon's lot would meet up here when it was open, and Gavin felt relieved when they turned up after their lunch, ten minutes later.

Zarok was stationed outside the door, which was partially open. Gideon had a look that said it all. He had his prey as good as captured.

'Where's your goofy little friends?' demanded Gideon sizing him up.

'Hiya Gideon. I just wanted to say, I am sorry we disrupted your science lesson. I don't have anything against you and I would like to make new friends while I am at Higglesdon Wick.' Josh looked scornful. *Boy was this kid green,* he thought.

'Really? Is that so! Well, if you show us what's behind yer sunglasses, I might consider it. Now you see, us lot usually meet with our friends right here, so why don't you come in with us and you can get to know us?!' offered Gideon slimily, winking at his guffawing mates. Gideon pushed Zarok into the dark room and as he did so, whispered to Montgomery, 'We'll nick his sunglasses as collateral!' But as they entered the dark box room, they had a surprise in store, literally.

Gavin sprang upon Gideon like an unrestrained lion, while Lee and Raj grabbed Diggory and Josh, taking them by surprise and throwing them to the back.

Reubin was on the scene in seconds, hauling Zarok out. He was followed by his friends who forced a near escapee (in the form of Diggory) back in. With all the boys pushing their weight against the door, Gavin locked it and the five calmly sauntered off. With that done, they could enjoy the afternoon now. Zarok looked really happy.

'Nice work Zarok!' winked Gavin.

'Crawb up!' clapped Reubin.

But now Mrs Bell appeared on the way to the PE block looking a little flustered. She wore her chunky knit scarf tightly round her as it had got chilly.

'I have been looking for you boys!' she said, looking directly at Zarok.

'I see the new boy has made firm friends very quickly!' she added with a tone of icy sarcasm.

'Although you have walked right in and joined lessons with us today, Zar…Zork? We must sort out your paperwork. Please come and see me in my office at the end of the afternoon!' Mrs Bell ordered curtly.

'See to it he does, Gavin!' she finished brusquely, marching off.

'Holy Moley!' exclaimed Raj.

'Yikes!' said Gavin. 'Well, we won't go, of course, Zarok! PE as usual! And after that we'll ride this out as long as possible!'

'Job done!' said Reubin cheerfully, slapping Zarok on the back.

CHAPTER TWELVE

SHOWCASING OF THE USA PROJECTS BEGINS

Oh dear! P.E. had not gone down well. Not just because it wasn't football, which the boys preferred. (Today, it was to be basketball, which was held inside a pleasant new sports hall that had been especially laid out for it.) The boys had gotten changed into their P.E. kits. Zarok needed to keep his legs covered and so wore leggings for this purpose. Having no P.E. kit, he borrowed shorts from the lost property box to wear over them, and continued to keep his hoodie and sunglasses on. Mr Ball was 'on the ball' and raring to go.

'Come on! Hurry up slowcoaches!' he yelled, as he jogged on the spot pumping his arms. As soon as the boys emerged he shouted, 'Warm up jog! Quick pace! Once around the hall!' And when that was done he ordered, 'Grab a ball from the rack and dribble it all the way! Come on Raj! Keep that ball going! Nice Gavin and Reubin! Keep it up Josh! That's good!'

But then Mr Ball stopped short, with his whistle poised by his mouth. *Who the devil was that boy without the proper kit?* For Mr Ball, turning up for P.E. with no kit, or an inadequate one, was the crime of the century.

'You boy! Stop right there!' hollered Mr Ball, before blowing his whistle shrilly. The whole proceedings ground to a halt. Diggory nudged Gideon and was looking forward to seeing what would happen next.

'Damn! They got out!' Gavin whispered to Reubin, stung. (It was the caretaker, Mr Bucket, who had hauled them out.)

'Do us a favour. We couldn't get rid of dem so easy bruv…'

'You Diggory! Sniggering are you? Face the wall at the back!'

'You boy! Yes you, next to Gavin! Name?!'

'Zarok,' said Zarok sheepishly, as Gideon and Josh stifled their giggles, stuffing hankies into their mouths. Reubin waved a fleeting fist at them.

'Well, Zarok! What's the meaning of you turning up at my lesson looking like you've landed from outer space?' The line-up of boys tittered. Teach had a point?!

'Cat got your tongue? Get those sunglasses off at the double!'

'He can't! He's got photophobia!' protested Gavin.

'His photo will be all over the school bulletin if he doesn't remove them in my lesson!' replied Mr Ball with gusto. Poor Zarok was trembling like a leaf.

'Right! Get out of my session and sort your kit out properly! No hoodies!' And with that, Mr Ball blew his whistle extra hard and grabbed a ball to dribble, along with his class. Zarok practically ran out. *School was so hard*, he thought. He would much rather be at home with Gavin's dog, plus he felt very unwell. His skin felt dry and itchy. Going back in and revealing his skin, which was so emaciated it looked ultra-violet, was out of the question. So was removing his glasses and showing his luminous opaque eyes. Yet he couldn't let the boys down by going? *But what was that?* Zarok decided he could at least try to do some P.E. after all! There was an empty swimming pool adjacent to the basketball hall. He found a long sleeved T-shirt in the lost property box and a pair of goggles. *Perfect!* Zarok enjoyed himself so much in the school pool that he completely forgot about the time and where he was. Next thing, his head rose halfway from the water to espy a fuming Mr Ball! (At least the goggles disguised much of his face and his body was submerged!) A group of open-mouthed boys stood by the door.

'What do you think you're playing at boy?! Get out of that pool IMMEDIATELY!' Zarok got out as quickly as he could and cut a dash for the changing rooms. Gavin hurriedly deterred Mr Ball by pressing him enthusiastically about the school quarter-finals, a subject that would keep Mr Ball rooted to the spot for ages. By the time Mr Ball was on Zarok's tail, he was gone. In fact, Gavin had kept him in conversation for so long that both the changing rooms were empty! *This action from that confounded new kid could not go unpunished,* thought Mr Ball grimly, making a mental note to put it to the Head.

***

At around four thirty, Honour popped into the salon where Miriam worked to have her hair done, telling her friend, 'I'll treat myself to a blow-dry my dear!' Miriam hurried to bring her some coffee and biscuits.

'I'm so glad you've popped in for a natter!' she said. 'What a day! It's been non-stop.' A serious look flitted across Honour's handsome features.

'What is it, Honour?' asked Miriam, immediately recognising that something was up.

'Er…Well, on my way over here I saw our boys… (She always called them 'our boys', as if they were all family.) They were running up the hill as usual, but with the most curious looking kid. The weird thing is, I think I've seen him before! He may well be the one that tried to hitch a lift back from the concert with us, and then did a disappearing act!'

'Really! Thank you for that Honour!' said Miriam with lips pursed, which rather spoiled her lipstick. 'I take it you don't like the look of him?'

'Frankly, Miriam dear, no! I mean, he wears sunglasses in the middle of winter?!'

***

The next morning, the boys awoke in a sober mood. Drew heard in detail everything that had gone down on account of Zarok at the secondary school, and Terry and Greg had also been filled in, much to their delight. Though Greg, in particular, had really felt for Zarok. The three of them weren't the best at looking ahead; all they knew was they felt a bit uneasy. *Maybe there could be trouble ahead?* But there was something worse than the consequences at school. Zarok had revealed some very disquieting news the night before. He had made them sit down and keep calm, making sure that he told them when their appetites were full and they were, therefore, relaxed.

'Gavin and Drew. I'm going to get straight to the point!' drawled Zarok in his characteristic Southern lilt.

'Straight to the horse's mouth!' cheered Drew.

'Bite the bullet!' laughed Gavin, stretching out and flexing a bit. But Zarok looked unduly sad.

'What is it? Don't you like our school? I know; it's crap there, innit!' Zarok looked down clasping his hands.

'I'm not well…Dudes… I don't know if you've noticed but I'm ageing a little faster than you two.'

'Hey! I don't look that old in three months!' voiced Drew indignantly, looking in the mirror to check.

'I can't stay on your planet for long without in the end suffering ill effects. My breathing is a slight problem and will get worse. I have more than one set of breathing apparatus as it were. One is alright here, and has adapted. The other isn't.'

Gavin and Drew, who had moved in close to Zarok, now looked distraught.

'My skin is very itchy and sore. That is one symptom. My gut is bad. I'm so sorry, boys. I don't like to moan!'

'Yeah, you sound like my uncle at Christmas!' groaned Gavin, trying to lighten the atmosphere. But Zarok cut through it, as this was his life he was talking about.

'I will die if I stay here much longer!' he cried dramatically.

'Oh no Zarok! How long do you think you have got?!' muttered Drew, perplexed now. Zarok did look unusually overwrought!

'Don't die on us will you, Zarok!' lamented Gavin.

'About three months! I must find a way to get back to my own planet!' Poor Zarok started to sob. Gavin tenderly lifted his sunglasses, revealing a flaccid skin that looked more wrinkly than usual and lustreless eyes. He looked dire…

Then Drew pulled himself together.

'No probs! We will find a way to get you back to your own planet, Zarok! We've already started, haven't we?! Don't forget we are going to America! I mean, what luck is that?! Of course, you are coming with us!'

'Yes, Zarok. We've got our USA projects tomorrow, and you know we're going to use this trip to get you home! It's all good!'

'But how?!' lamented Zarok. 'Even if we get there, it could all be a dream. Really, I don't know what to do or how to do it myself!'

'We will find a way Zarok, I promise!' promised Gavin with a confidence he didn't completely own. While he went to clean his teeth, Drew gave Zarok a reassuring hug.

'Don't worry Zarok! Me n' Gavin, with the help of the Dogs o' Hell, can do anything!'

'Thankyou Drew' said Zarok sleepily, a faint smile on his face as he drifted off to sleep with some comfort to hang on to. He had good friends.

***

The next morning, the boys awoke feeling refreshed and hopeful, including Zarok. Today was the day of the USA project presentations, and the first step in their endeavours to get Zarok home. It was an important day! Miriam left just after the boys that morning to see if she could glance at her boy's apparently odd new friend. But, as usual, they met Terry n' Greg at the bus stop with Reubin, and Zarok caught up with them at the school gates. He had been feeling wan and a group of Hell Dogs first thing, was a bit much for him. However, he was really looking forward to the group presentations on America and anxious to learn what destinations would be selected, and who would go where! He ascertained that Gavin and Drew didn't really grasp just how big America was.

'Oi weirdo! Ditch the shades, it's freakin' January!' shouted Gideon to Zarok on his way in. Zarok hurried to join his friends who were mooching around in a bunch at the far side of the forefront recreation area. Greg and Terry patted him on the back as he entered the group.

'Soz to hear you're not well, Zarok' said Greg kindly, if not tactfully. Just then, someone new skipped up to the group. It was Geeta who was in Gavin's class.

'Here comes your girlfriend, Gav. Members only!' scowled Terry.

'Get to your own school!' challenged Geeta loftily.

'I want to talk with Gavin a minute on his own,' said Geeta importantly. 'Whahay!' The boys teased as Gavin took three steps out of the group and merely said, 'Wot?' to her. She pulled out her mobile and showed Gavin an image. The image was a dead ringer for Zarok.

'There's a mini twitter storm about an odd looking boy at a concert,' she confided. 'Some trolls have focused on it after this footage was on the news. Some are saying they reckon it's an alien! The thing is Gavin, he looks a little bit like Zarok! That's if he didn't wear sunglasses; the little nose and mouth anyway…' She paused, looking deeply at Gavin who deliberately assumed a casual expression. But Geeta liked Gavin and wanted to help him. She'd been shocked at the bullying of their new classmate, Zarok.

'Er, thanks Geeta,' replied Gavin uneasily. 'I s'pose I see what you mean.'

Gavin pounced on his group, turning back to shout at Geeta, 'Don't show anyone will ya!'

'Flippin' heck,' he gasped, moving in on them and relaying the news quickly.

'A storm in a teacup which will become a very big storm!' commented Lee wisely.

'And a very big cup!' added Greg, wincing at Zarok.

'This is a Red Alert situation for the Hell Dogs!' said Gavin importantly.

'This stuff will be round the school like wildfire. Noone knows he's an alien yet, but it will now be the question on everyone's lips…I'm sorry Zarok. You'll have to go home today until we find out what they're all saying, and…' Mrs Bell intruded upon them abruptly. None of them had noticed her coming and they hoped she had not heard the word '*alien*'.

'You two were supposed to come to my office after school yesterday!' she scolded.

'Not me, just Zarok!' protested Gavin.

'It seems…' Mrs Bell hesitated, looking round at the bunch of boys.

'Get to your own school, Terry, Greg and Drew!' she ordered briskly.

'It seems there are questions to be answered around Zarok's admission here! That's all I'm saying for now. I want you in my office a good ten minutes before school commences!' she emphasised with a wagging finger.

'That does it!' moaned Gavin. 'I'm afraid you will *definitely* have to go home, Zarok.'

'Looks like we will probably have to face the music for you,' offered up Reubin miserably. He didn't want to get into trouble so near the trip. 'More life, more strength yana…' Reubin looked uneasy for them though.

'Don't worry. It's Gav's fault, not yours…' said Raj sycophantically.

So off poor Zarok went, waving goodbye and dragging his feet. It was a disaster as first thing, in no time at all, Gavin, Reubin, Lee and Raj were hauled out of their computer literacy class. They were going to face the wrath of who…? Baldy?

Luckily, it was only Mrs Bell. Mr Baldwin was supposed to be coming, but had meeting after meeting that day.

'When in doubt, deny!' rasped Gavin to his comrades.

'OK. How do you know Zarok, Gavin?!' Mrs Bell began.

'I don't miss!' objected Gavin, looking wild-eyed and feeling trapped.

'I suppose you don't know Zarok either!' said Mrs Bell, turning to Reubin.

'No! No miss!' swore Reubin, eyes cast down to the floor.

'And you Lee? And Raj – is Zarok a mate of yours?'

'Yes, I mean no!' said Raj. 'I mean yes; I'm the same as the others, like I don't know him!'

'Let me try again. Are you sure that none of you know Zarok?! You seem to be very pally with him!' pressed Mrs Bell.

'No! We met him in the playground, Miss. He was new so we befriended him!' insisted Gavin with believable sincerity. Mrs Bell relented a little bit.

'Is it true he turned up to genuinely enrol at our school?! We've only got his word for it!' she pushed, scanning them for any giveaway expressions.

'It's true. Didn't Baldy tell you?' asked Raj innocently. The others sighed with disbelief. Raj had messed up good and proper.

'How would you know Mr Baldwin recommended him!' boomed Mrs Bell.

'I didn't. I just assumed you would have to pass his admission with the Head', stammered poor Raj. The others looked assuaged. He'd saved it.

'I did not ADMIT him! Neither did Miss Speakwell! Where is he?'

'He's gone home– to his yard. He had a headache Miss,' replied a pained Reubin.

'Why does that not surprise me?! Do you know, you could have bought a frankly dangerous youth into our school!'

'We didn't bring him in, Miss! He approached us in the playground and we tried to carry out the school code, to do a kindness a day!' said Lee, smiling ingratiatingly. Mrs Bell paused for a very long time, the colour draining from her gaily painted face.

'So none of you know him!' she sighed at a loss.

'No, no Miss! We met him in the playground! He was in school uniform and everything! His mum couldn't be there with him!' replied Reubin sincerely.

'OK…OK,' she said, holding up her hands in a gesture of surrender.

'But there are more mysteries around this and it might not be the last time I bring you back here. Do any of you have his phone number, his address or email?!' she asked, trying for the last time through gritted teeth.

'No Miss! We just met him in the play…'

'Enough!' cried Mrs Bell. 'This is potentially a very serious matter. Now get to class!'

'Phew!' went Gavin when they had all got out of there! 'That was a close call. Good one all of you…Deny, deny, deny!' he ratified confidently.

'What did you say Gavin?' demanded Mrs Bell, her head swooping round the door.

'I said we denied our involvement, Miss!' replied Gavin coolly.

'Whew…Lon dil' ting' mumbled Reubin. But Mrs Bell had caught it.

'I beg your pardon?' Reubin assumed an expression of surprise.

'Indeed, it will be a long-deal-thing Reubin!' she responded purposefully.

'As much as I love you guys, I don't want this trouble,' said Lee. 'I want to get to my lessons on time and do my work well. Also, if I don't, my dad will kill me!'

'So will mine!' seconded Raj. Gavin and Reubin looked cynical for a moment. Then they remembered, school could be pretty good. After all, there were the projects that afternoon.

'I'm sorry Lee. You really are good and we need you in our gang. You just join us when you want to OK? I know you like doing your homework… You too Raj. You're brilliant too. The Zarok thing gets a bit much sometimes, doesn't it?!'

'It's OK. I just don't want to fail. *Our stuff* mustn't step over my lessons!'

'Or cramp my style,' put in Raj.

'You haven't got any style to cramp!' carped Reubin, giving him a not so friendly shove. 'You nearly ruined Drew's work there doops!'

***

That afternoon, just before the USA Project Presentations took place, Gavin saw a familiar figure sidling up to him in the playground. It was a good classmate of his called Xavier who had been ill and off school for weeks.

'Hey Xavier! Yay! It's Xavier!' he shouted out, greeting his friend with a friendly punch. 'You alright mate?!'

'Yeah I'm OK now. I'm over my tonsillitis!' he replied with a grin. Gavin's pals, who were friendly with him too, came over to welcome him back.

'Geezah!' cried Reubin. *'Wah gwaan?'*

'What about the presentations this afternoon!' suggested Lee, anxious to go.

'Lucky I'm back in time for all that, but I've not been involved,' explained Xavier, looking a bit put out.

'Don't worry,' said Gavin putting his arm round him as the group made their way to the school hall, 'you can join in with us! The more the merrier!' Then, as they lined up in the corridor, Raj pointed out Gideon's gang, who seemed to have an added contingent.

'We *need* Xavier too!' voiced Raj urgently.

'Cripes! I never thought of that!' copped Gavin, slapping his hand to his head in despair.

'Of course… I doubt it's really about who has the best ideas…It's about strength in numbers!'

'I agree,' said Lee. 'How can they turn down a proposal when one group is a majority! There's five of us with Xavier, and Gideon's got…' The boys gaped down the line to see Gideon preside over Bradley, Cosimo, Dent, Basil and Giles, as well as his own crew. That made nine!

'Where do they wanna go?' asked Xavier.

'It doesn't matter about that!' determined Gavin. 'Get your mates, Jake and Sergiusz and Dan to come over to our side! Quick!'

'But they think I'm joining up with them. They don't know you're twisting my arm to join with you lot!'

'Even better!' chipped in Reubin, who was very tall and towered over Xavier.

'Get 'em over 'ere, and we'll join forces. Don't make it obvious!' he added.

So Xavier slipped out of the line to accost his friends, while Gavin also stepped out to surreptitiously beckon them over.

Gideon, however, saw him and yelled, 'Ha ha!' They all wanna go to L.A. and I bet their project is heaps better than yours!'

Gideon's cronies joined in the jeering. But Jake, Sergiusz and Dan not only admired Gavin, they were also worried about their own numbers too. So they casually moved up the line to join Gavin and co., bravely sticking their fingers up at Gideon's gang as they went.

'Did I hear you say, 'Ha ha'?' Reubin shouted back at to them.

'Come on!' said Lee, frustrated. 'We need to focus on our project!'

'We planned to go to L.A.,' stated Jake. 'And I'm the group leader!'

'You're not the group leader anymore!' reproached Gavin.

'I know,' conceded Jake. 'But we've done a lot of research on our project!'

'Like we haven't!' retorted Gavin. 'But don't worry. L.A. is right next to Arizona, so we'll get both of them in!' soothed Gavin more kindly.

'Yes, we can cover two states!' came in Xavier glad for a resolution; he hadn't wanted to dog out his friends. And so it was settled. The rank of Gavin's group had swelled, and so they walked in tall. As far as numbers were concerned, they would give as commanding a project as their rivals.

'Yah! You haven't rehearsed it!' Gideon sniped to Gavin as all the pupils filed in. The classes took their chairs, which lined the entire width of the hall, from top to bottom. Along the far side of it, where the parameters were painted for sports purposes, benches had been positioned lengthways. These were reserved for the top classes of Higglesdon Wick

Juniors. Some of the teachers were to be stationed around the hall, and some at a table in the corner. It all looked very formal!

The children chattered among themselves until Mr Baldwin himself rang a bell. This was the signal for everyone to quieten down. By this time, Higglesdon Wick Juniors were seated beside Mr Jackson, as were a good many teachers, including Miss Hope, Mr Bunsen and Mr Anderson and even Mr Ball, who looked distracted when he did anything that wasn't to do with P.E.

'Welcome everyone to our USA Project Presentations! I hope you have all done your research well, not only to grant us an enjoyable session, but to help us determine which of the destinations will go through to be chosen for our USA trips. Good luck to all of you! Now, without further ado, Mr Anderson is going to chair this afternoon's proceedings!'

Mr Baldwin, who had devoured more than his fair share of lunch, gratefully sat down to hand over to Mr Anderson. Gavin was sad that Zarok wasn't with them. In fact, Zarok was glad to be at home taking refuge in the garden shed, where he had stayed since Mrs Beak's arrival to do some cleaning; and no doubt scan under the beds!

'Hello everyone! Let me just say that every pupil here has been passed for the USA trips, upon parental consent, regardless of whether they have siblings in the upper school. However, if you do have brothers and sisters across both schools, we will endeavour to keep you together, unless any special consideration arises. We will have our first years at Higglesdon Wick Secondary putting forward their pitches. Nevertheless, we expect them to have taken input from the juniors in their choice of destination. So with that, let's get on with it folks! First up are Verity, Sian, Belinda and Nabila, Aleksy and Rowena.' The six girls took to the front of the hall giggling and rustling their papers. Belinda and Nabila were not the best of friends with the other two, but they'd agreed on the destination. The most confident, if not bossy, of them began.

'We've decided that we want to go to Disneyland!' declared Verity importantly, projecting her voice and engaging her audience. A raucous cheer went up. Mr Anderson groaned inwardly. He'd dreaded this, yet knew it would doubtless be a popular choice.

'We want to go to the sleeping Beauty Castle and think everyone would enjoy experiencing its magic, and I want to meet Mickey Mouse in person!' said Verity in one breath.

'We are all agreed that Disneyland is the most popular destination as it's termed the happiest place on Earth and I wanna go to the sorcerers workshop!' added Sian perfunctorily. Another cheer went up.

'There are loads of things to do in Disneyland!' went on Belinda, 'which is in er…California. You could stay there a month, no forever, and never get bored!'

'That's all good girls, but we did ask you to include an educational bent in the presentation of your choice of destination!' pressed Mr Anderson with a smile.

'Yes Sir! The Disneyland Resort is a real one, actually under Walt Disney. It has been open since 1955, which is a long time ago. That means it's a historical venue!' added Verity.

'You can visit the Disney gallery and take notes. You can also go on the Disney California Story Tour. There is not a single pupil here who does not know something of the stories, and there are other attractions to do with popular big film franchises. Stories help us with literacy and harness our imagination!' went on Aleksy inspirationally.

'My turn!' grumbled Sian. 'It's educational to go on the Big Thunder Mountain Railroad and the Golden Zephyr ride, which I think is a rollercoaster.'

'Why?' questioned Mr Anderson.

'Because it just is. Disneyland is a once in a lifetime experience and who wants to go there when your old and an adult?!' she replied, finishing to a round of applause.

'Very good girls! Any pictures?' asked Mr Anderson. Nabila, Aleksy and Rowena who had done their homework, handed photocopies to each row to pass round. These included over twenty attractions and places to stay, as well as special events and discounts. Meanwhile, they held up their trump card of a sizeable poster they had made, which included stuck on pictures of Disneyland and giant cartoon characters. Across the top was emblazoned in glitzy letters, 'Go Disney!' and 'Vote Disneyland!' It was just as well as they'd hardly got a word in edgeways. Mr Baldwin liked that touch and beamed from ear to ear. The first project, although scant on content, had got across due to its emotional appeal.

'Crikey!' whispered Gavin to Reubin. 'That's a hard act to follow!'

'Yeah, what rubbish it is really though! We're gonna do better than that dups!' he replied heartily. But Gavin was right. It was going to be hard to convince the pupils to go to a bleak desert in Arizona. Disneyland was its polar opposite!

***

CHAPTER THIRTEEN

GAVIN AND FRIENDS SHOWCASE THEIR USA PROJECT PROPOSAL

'OK! I don't want to hear anyone say, 'I want to go to this or that state because a family member lives there or has been there!' articulated Mr Anderson after the proposal of another class group, led by Noah, was rejected on the spot. Noah, Akmal, Roger and Dave had wanted to go to El Dorado to pan for gold. Apparently, Dave's uncle had wound up there once.

'Not only that, it's in South America. You didn't read the brief properly!'

The sea of pupils tittered nervously. It had sounded quite exciting…

'Great! If they're disqualified, all the more chances for us!' sniffed Gavin. He gave a thumbs up sign to Drew, Terry n' Greg, who were sat in the front row benches looking hopeful, anxious to see Gavin up there.

'Next up, Jocelyn's group!' called out Mr Anderson. 'Oh! I see there's a lot of you going for this one.' The girls ran up to the front and fanned out in a row.

'We have Jocelyn, Clair, Ife, Bethany, Reena, Melissa, Hazine and Geeta. You may begin. No need to fiddle with your hair Hazine,' said Mr Anderson.

'I'm the project leader and the thing all of us have in common is that we would like to go skiing! It is the middle of winter and skiing is not something we can take advantage of in our own country. Probably most of us have never had the chance to go skiing…'

'I have and so has…' exclaimed Verity, which came out a bit too loudly.

'We know *you* have!' cut in Melissa scathingly. Oh dear, it had been a good beginning. 'My daaays…She's such a bossy boots that girl…'

'Shutup…' hissed Jocelyn, while Clair took one step forward to say the next bit.

'We think skiing is educational because you can learn a new skill and also get fit at the same time.' Mr Ball looked on approving and nodded his head ferociously.

'Here are some of the places that you can go skiing,' said Bethany rather woodenly. 'In New England, you can go to Mohawk mountain and ski areas; Ski Sundown and New Hartford' and ski…Corn…I can't read the next bit.'

Clair hurriedly took over at this point. 'In Maine, you can go ski at Big Rock, Mars Hill, the Lonesome Pine trails, Fort Kent, Sugarloaf and the Carrabassett Valley!' she read out brightly.

'Er…Can we avoid lists of places, please!' commented Mr Anderson.

'We haven't finished, Sir!' protested Ife, who was next. 'In Pennsylvania, you can go to Blue Knob All Seasons Resort.'

Gideon's gang began sniggering, 'Blue knob, eh? Heh, heh…' they chortled. Ife cracked on unperturbed.

'You can go to Bears Creek Mountain Resort there too, and in Ohio, you can ski at Bellefontaine on the Mad River Mountain.'

'Wow!' enthused Gavin and his friends, who were impressed. That did sound good! Despite themselves, they gave a round of applause.

'History?!' quizzed Mr Anderson.

'Yes, Mr Anderson. I'm doing the next bit!' said Melissa, bracing herself. 'You can go skiing in Montana…' She met Mr Anderson's eye and decided to try and refrain from lists.

'Montana has a diverse terrain from the Rocky mountains to the Great Plains. It is Big Sky country. The glacier national park passes into Canada. There are snow-capped mountains…'

'Bah, you don't say…' jeered Diggory as Melissa raised her voice over him…

'And lakes and Alpine Trails…And you can go to the Bear Paw Ski Bowl…'

Reena nudged Melissa.

'You can go to Big Sky Resort and get a big sky resort lift ticket. You can visit the Lost Trail Powder Mountain. The capital is Helena and the neighbouring states of Wyoming. Idaho and North and South Dakota.' She was giggling as she finished.

'Reena?' called Mr Anderson.

'If you want to go skiing in New Orleans…you can't. The closest in Cloudmont is Northern Eastern Alabama or the Crystal Mountain in Washington USA. In Washington, on a clear day, you are surrounded by mountains of white, oversized, dormant volcanoes…'

'Yeah like, let's go skiing on a volcano!' quipped Josh.

'And you can go to the summit of Snogqualmie…Um… That's it!'

The room thundered out their applause. It was the best one so far. When it had died down, Mr Anderson spoke.

'I can see there is quite a bit of research in that. More geography than history, so with my being a geography teacher, I should be pleased with that. Any thoughts Mr Baldwin?' Mr Baldwin made a wavering motion with his hand.

'If I may say something!' volunteered Mr Jackson.

'I think some of my class would like to go skiing, and may I congratulate you on an almost flawless presentation girls. Well done!' The girls tripped away beaming. In fact, it had been rather stilted, but they had crammed a lot of info in there.

'Next up, I believe, is 'Connors Crew' as it says here.'

Connor was from the other class, and there was a mix of girls and boys in his group. Many were part of a dance troupe and some of them acted or sang in local outfits. It was, therefore, a sizeable group with a good chance of clinching where they wanted to go. Among them were Jirani, Ndidi, Halina, Jessica, Dimitri, Christian and Melody.

'I'm Project leader! We decided we'd like to go to Hollywood, but we wanna go to New York too, so if possible, we'd like to do both. New York first!' addressed Connor, his arms outstretched. Then, surprisingly, four of his group burst into a very entertaining song and dance routine about New York. It went down a storm. Once the clapping was over, a striking girl named Ndidi continued.

'Did you know, there are 261 landmarks in N.Y.?! Think of that?! Many of you will have heard of the iconic Statue of Liberty, Wall Street or Fifth Avenue. In New York, there is something for everyone! The island borough of Manhattan is at the Big Apple's core... Today, we want to persuade you to take that journey with us! I ap-peal' to you!' she laughed.

A boy named Christian waddled on, wearing a plump foam apple that encompassed his body from the head to his knees. This went down a treat. Next was Melody, who dared to take to the stage at the end of the hall.

'Personally, I want to witness famous places like Times Square, Central Park and the Empire State Building, so that I can say, 'I've been there,' and feel part of history! (At this point, Melody waved her arms about, gesticulating gracefully.) But you might like to forgo downtown places – where you can visit Chinatown in Washington Square, The Intrepid Sea Air and Space museum or the dead famous Guggenheim museum – and instead hit Coney Island seaside resort! New York, so good they named it twice!' she yelled.

Then, all twelve of them suddenly sported New York T-shirts as they launched into a brilliant song and dance routine with seaside props. It was original material they had worked on too. The school hall erupted into roars of enthusiasm with cheers of 'Bravo' and Hooray!' Gavin and his friends couldn't help but join in.

'Drat!' said Reubin to Gavin, his eyes still glued to the spectacle.

'They're pros man! They'll definitely get it, I'm tellin' ya…'

'You gotta give it to them Reubin. They deserve to go to N.Y.!'

'Yana! That was bad, bruv!' agreed Reubin reluctantly. 'Dey got sass…'

All the teachers gave a standing ovation and when the applause died down, Mr Anderson said: 'A big well done! That was thoroughly entertaining! This isn't a talent contest, but suffice to say, your enthusiasm for New York was contagious. Right everybody! We are going to take a short break now! There is orange squash and cake, as I understand it, laid on in the canteen. Go enjoy, and after that we will resume the projects. And I mean a short break!' he yelled, as the pupils scrambled for the door in a pretty dysfunctional fashion. This was thirsty work!

Gavin, Drew, Terry n' Greg, Reubin, Raj, Lee, Xavier, Jake, Dan and Sergiusz, stood huddled in a corner of the canteen gratefully munching their cake.

'They shunt let Josh go, he's bare loaded!' carped Terry.

'Isn't he Persian or Arabian and African too, Josh? His endz is bad! Anyway, he lives in a castle practically. I heard he's got gold taps and champagne toothpaste in his bathroom!' added Greg ruefully. (Josh's house was surrounded by a turreted high wall.)

'He's a bit of a neek though. He's already learning business studies! And he's up Gideon's butt,' relayed Terry with a grimace.

'Gideon and Diggory ain't even that rich; they act it to suck up to him!'

'Shut up about Josh! This is our chance to sort our show!' cried Gavin.

'My dad knows his dad and his cat wears a designer coat,' revealed Sergi.

'The carp in his pond have their own private yachts,' grinned Raj warming to the subject.

'Ha ha! Nice one Raj. This is yum orange!' said Terry. 'Better than our school's!'

'Tezza?!' Gavin's comrades were exasperating him.

'It's good cake too! Mmm…buttercream,' drooled Raj.

'Mmm…jam sponge!' approved Lee, licking crumbs from his lips.

'I got nutty bits!' Reubin crammed the cake in his mouth in one go.

'What do you think this is – a cookery appreciation society?' mocked Gavin.

'Look guys! Get serious! That lot were good. I don't know how we can compete!'

'And they just kept getting better!' groaned Terry, spot on.

'You're on the money, Terry!' said Greg ruefully. 'I wish we could join you in your presentation, Gavin!'

'I'm not being funny, but you wouldn't make it better!' came in Reubin speaking plainly.

'It's not because of you dups, but the content! I mean how are we going to make a frickin' desert look interesting?!' raved Reubin. 'We're only doing it coz of Zarok! *An' we need to beat dem bad!*'

'S***!' Gavin clapped his hand over Reubin's mouth, looking horrified.

'Zarok?' questioned Xavier as Reubin visibly withered…

'Oh, he's just a kid that came to our school' explained Lee breezily, coming to the rescue.

'He was quite clever and when he heard about the projects he suggested that we try and put forward the Grand Canyon. Like eejits, we went along with it!'

The boys had no time to think of ideas to improve on their presentation apart from one thing, which Gavin put out there in the nick of time.

'No one mention Route 666 or The Devil's Highway, or all bets are off!'

'It's called route 191 now anyway,' sniffed Lee.

'Don't matter, same thing – they'll know that and throw it out!'

'Why?' asked Greg.

'Because the numbers six hundred and sixty six are synonymous with 'The Beast' in the Bible, and so it will offend some people!' enlightened Raj.

'Yes! Like wot's a devil. It's not the sort of thing that's going to sell it to the teachers!' confirmed Gavin.

***

Everyone filed back into the hall expectantly. An air of excitement was in the air. The showcasing had allowed everyone to dream, and what's more, dreams would be turned into reality.

'Settle down please! Next up is Gideon...and his friends.' Mr Anderson decided to forgo reading out 'Gideon's Gang' in front of Mr Baldwin.

Gideon's gang with his extras slouched on and stood in a tight bunch behind him, hands in their pockets.

'Hi fans! I'm Gideon and we want to go toooo...Miami! And we want you to come for the ride with us!' Gideon pointed both fingers at his audience theatrically, attempting to bring some zip into his performance.

'South Beach –check! Crowds hanging poolside- check! Rollerblading down Ocean Drive–check!' Gideon was prowling up and down the stage, reckoning he would bring some cool to the proceedings. It was a bit risky in front of Baldwin, but it was going down well. He wasn't afraid of working it after Connor.

'Alright, alright,' muttered Mr Anderson.

'Designer boutiques galore – check! (The ranks of children that were swelling the hall all began to chant 'Check!' along with him, egged on by Diggory.)

'OK Mr Anderson, you get the picture! I'm going to let my right-hand man, Diggory, take over. Take it away, Dig!'

'Come with us to Miami and soon you'll be taking a stroll past tanned reality TV stars! Check! We bet you can pose for a selfie with them. Check! Yes, it's top models sauntering along golden sands, and you too can live the dream! You can go to a whole design district and shop til' you drop!'

Many of the children sat up agog. This indeed sounded like the fantasy holiday! Glorious beaches and at this time of year?!

'Relevance!' reminded Mr Anderson. Diggory looked at him pop-eyed.

'Oh yeah, we got history and geography too!' claimed Josh, getting ready to strut his stuff next.

'Big ups Josh!' yelped Gideon, giving a thumbs up to the crowd.

'You can experience little Havana after Fidel Castro came to power in 1959 and hundreds of Cubans fled to Miami, but if you get sick of that, you can get to see live police chases po-po fans!' Montgomery pushed him out the way.

'There are countless things to do; it's not all sunbathing, swimming and lounging in the sand. You can go to Magic City where it's said it is fast on its feet when it comes to celebrations! Each spring there is a spring *latino* Miami that struts it's stuff at Carnival Miami! A carnival – and we'd be in time to see it!

It's ten days of beauty pageants, music festivals and performing DJs, costumes, street food and amazing culture to learn of!' He finished by meeting Anderson's eye, before rousing his audience with a last resounding 'CHECK!!'

'That's it. We're done! Blink and you'll miss it!' winked Gideon as he sauntered off with his gang in tow. 'Smashed it!' he mumbled audibly.

His latest auxiliary members hadn't done much in the way of vocals. But they had busied themselves by setting up a few parasols, which were really umbrellas, thrown a bucket of sand over the stage and strewn some beach towels over it all during proceedings. A show of hands went up and the children began to chant 'Miami!' The teachers were scribbling notes. That looked promising.

'That was a spirited performance boys. A bit unconventional, yet possibly in the spirit of Miami! I especially liked the last bit. To witness a carnival could be really marvellous, although I would be a bit afraid of children getting lost in the crowds. Well delivered!'

'Top that losers!' snarled Gideon to Gavin (who did not want to admit that he liked their presentation and would like to go to Miami too!)

'Yes but not as much as Arizona!' whispered Raj, not wanting Gavin to lose heart.

'How we gonna top Magic City, bredda?!' mouthed a downcast Reubin. The boys straightened their ties and gathered up their papers. But before they took to the stage, they had a trick up their sleeve!

'If we may draw the curtains, Mr Anderson?'

'Surely boys,' answered Mr Anderson obligingly. Raj was setting up a home projector. It was old fashioned but would do. It wasn't working too well on the undulating red curtains, and Gideon and his followers began to laugh out loud, 'putting on' extra mirth to boot.

'Don't worry boys! There's a standing white screen behind there at the back. Now find it and hurry up and assemble it!' assured Mr Anderson.

'Memba mi tell yu, we gonna beat dem bad!' hissed Reubin.

The first image was now up. It was a scene of the Grand Canyon in all its glory.

'That, is where we want you to go!' impelled Gavin, gesturing to the lovely expanse. 'This is nothing more, and nothing less than the Grand Canyon in fantabulous Arizona. For those who wish to view this amazing natural wonder of the universe, our journey would best start in Las Vegas – and we'd travel from there in just over a couple of hours! We would go through Boulder City and over the Colorado Bridge to Arizona.' Raj was clicking away, presenting his pictures to 'Oohs and Ahhs!'

Now it was Reubin's turn. He smiled ingratiatingly. 'Go some places with fake effects and sets that have been mentioned here today, and lose! Cruisers are losers! There's nothing plastic about this fantasy set! It's real! It's poppin'! It's a geographical wonder that affords spectacular views that can't just be recreated anywhere! It's a photographer's paradise!'

Lee cleared his throat and walked on ready to deliver some baloney now as best he could.

'Ahem. Ladies and gentlemen! There is nothing quite like Arizona! Yes, you may say it's just a desert…'

'Let's go to Death Valley while we're at it, aye? That'll be fun!' yelled out Gideon.

'Don't scrape in douche-bag!' yelled Terry, unable to contain himself.

'Be quiet or get out! Insolence!' bellowed Mr Baldwin, who had taken a bit of shut-eye. Lee took a deep breath.

'Arizona is home to dozens of noteworthy roads, byways and historic loops; perfect for touring and enjoying wholesome road trips! You can find hairpin turns and steep cliffs and ever changing scenery. Everywhere you go, you see incredible panoramic views. Like, you can go to Arizona's Cabeza Prieta; a national wildlife refuge.'

'I bet you all like animals, and in Arizona you can find amazing...'

'Bison...' put in Gavin, just in case. 'What Lee's tryin' to tell you is that it's an adventure of a lifetime!'

'We need to talk L.A.,' whispered Jake urgently.

'Get a move on boys! You're running out of time and we have to be fair to all of you!' admonished Mr Anderson curtly.

'Quick! Move it on,' rasped Reubin to Lee, who was doing well.

'Er...There is absolutely nothing quite like the um... Coronado Scenic Byway! It has been proven to be one of the most exciting places on Earth for those who love adventure!'

'Isn't that the Devil's Highway?' mumbled Mr Anderson to Miss Hope abstractedly.

'Yes Sir! We are talking about a prehistoric colonial trail! You can take a one to ten day ride to the breathtaking Black Hills... It's history and geography all in one!'

'L.A...L.A.!' squealed Jake, jumping up and down now. Brandishing his script, he was overwrought with frustration! Lee turned to him blankly.

'Jake would like to take a route out of Arizona at some point and visit L.A. It is, after all, the next US State and everyone has heard about 'The City of Angels!' But after that, I mean before that, you can go from Alpine to Morenci and experience a hundred miles of amazing landscapes and expanses of nature that you'll remember for the rest of your life! There's more than enough history to shake a stick at and, therefore, our destination fits the brief in a way that the others do not! Not only that, we have a clear US State to visit' finished Lee, glaring at the ski girls.

Raj finished with an incredible picture of a giant cactus glowing in a sunset desert. The boys stood in a line and gave awkward little bows, while the packed hall of pupils went wild, cheering and clapping. Gavin, Reubin and Xavier egged them on with spread-eagled palms. For some reason, the boys had truly captured the children's imagination.

'I want to go there!' squealed a girl called Stacey from the Juniors. 'Me too!' yelled her friends. 'We love that one!'

'Big ups Gavin and Reubin! Big ups!' yelled Terry and Greg milking it.

'What a load o' rubbish!' shouted Montgomery over the din.

'Three-Two-One RUBBISH!' egged on Gideon (directing his fingers at the assembly.)

'Rubbish man!' echoed Josh dutifully.

'I have to say that was very well done boys! I like to see that you've taken it seriously. Certainly, we have both history and geography taken up. However, some places you mention are rather dubious and may not be as nice as they make out in the tourist brochures!'

'We want to go to the Coronado Scenic Byway!' shouted Terry n' Greg. They were infectious! Their class copied them, joining in! The presentations were not over by any means. Next up was Gavin's neighbouring class. A group of girls from it were also set on going skiing. They gave a first class presentation on it and had even arranged a full itinerary for the duration of the holiday that would include other activities for the most adventurous, outdoorsy pupils. The teachers were visibly impressed. The content and delivery was excellent.

Then came a group intent on going to California. With mentions of the Golden Gate Bridge, imaginations were stirred. Surfing, kayaking, paddle boarding and Segway riding were audibly popular. So were jet pack flights, sport fishing and whale watching. The children managed to convey more than just a beach image, but a cultural and sporty and innovative message. They left the audience inspired and half desperate to get on a plane (as this was now freezing January) and fly to California, there and then! Gideon and his mates looked crestfallen, as the beach spiel had been miles better than theirs! They had made Gideon's look shallow! Reubin was watching them and openly pointed his finger with a 'mimed' laugh.

'Thank you everyone for participating in what has been a pleasant and successful afternoon!' said Mr Baldwin. 'Thank you Mr Anderson, for managing events! A big thank you to the canteen staff for laying on a nice tea for us! Plus, let us *all* remember Chester Cash, ahem… Cass, in our prayers when we go home tonight! Our staff will be getting our heads together to decide on the four destinations, and who will be going where. It will take two to three days for the results to be verified! Good luck all of you once again!'

Thank goodness Mr Baldwin hadn't gone on…

'You've done us out of our L.A. presentation!' lamented Jake, sounding so stressed that he looked as if he was going to burst into tears.

'Lee mentioned it!' answered Gavin shortly and gravely.

'No?! He should have just handed over to me next!' cried poor Jake.

'I am sorry. There was not enough time!' said Lee diplomatically.

Reubin grabbed Jake by the shoulder.

'Look Jake. He said sorry. One day mate, you will understand that it's important!' offered up Reubin, before shaking his head and mooching off.

'Aye?!' remarked Xavier quizzically on his friend's behalf. He hadn't meant it to come to this. Gavin had basically trashed his chances of L.A.!

Then Raj said…

'If they choose us Jake, L.A. will be part of the package. We will get to go there too! After all it was said in the presentation!'

'L.A wasn't discussed at all. The teachers heard naff all about it!' he yelped.

'What do you like about L.A. anyway?!' demanded Lee more cryptically.

'It's cool there. Um…I dunno really. It's just what we chose and worked on!'

'Exactly! You will see that the Coronado Scenic Trail is heaps better than ole L.A!'

'Really – Lee, Gavin?'

'Yes really! You'll be glad you came. Plus you'll be with us!'

Gavin took to his heels, hands in his pockets and blazer lapels turned up, the second he was through the school gates.

'One step closer to the Devil's Highway…and getting our Zarok safely home!' affirmed Gavin to Reubin.

'Job done, comrade!' came back Reubin, his fist clenched and his knuckles meeting Gavin's in a gesture of solidarity. Just then, Terry n' Greg, Raj and Lee came rushing up to them, jumping on them and punching the air.

'Yay! Bet we did it!' they cried. And with that, the Hell Dogs raced up the road whirling their bags around and around to whoops of premature joy.

CHAPTER FOURTEEN
STEPS BEFORE THE TRIP

It was Saturday, the most glorious day of the week. The Dogs of Hell had met up in the afternoon and realising it was too cold to hold a meeting at the allotment, had decided to play football in the park with some of the local lads. Terry's dad had invited himself along to act as referee, the keen footie enthusiast that he was. The boys weren't worried that Zarok would feel left out.

Their alien friend was more than happy to hang out in Drew and Gavin's bedroom, tending his own collection of cactus plants. Not only that, he had a pile of Drew and Gavin's homework to get through. This was a task he not only enjoyed, but was exceptional at. And since the return of their laptop, he had learnt so much. He enjoyed learning everything possible about his host planet.

In the meantime, Gavin and Drew were in their teachers' best books due to their schoolwork going from below average to excellent!

Later in the afternoon, the boys returned from an enjoyable game, grubby and glowing. Soon Drew, Gavin, Reubin, Terry n' Greg and Raj were sat around their kitchen table. Someone else was also there, and that was Billie, who had set herself up painting.

'Hello' she said. 'You must be quiet, I'm concentrating boys,' sounding just like her mother.

'Oh no, we will not!' Gavin said, rounding on her. He began to clear away her paints, then topped the box with her jam jar of water.

'Don't! Go away!' she cried, reaching out for her materials hopelessly.

'Soz Billie! I'm afraid you gotta go now! We got urgent business to attend to!' Billie looked as though she was going to cry.

'But I got here first!' she protested, her voice quavering.

'And we got here second!' trumped Terry. Then, as Billie reluctantly left the room, dragging her feet as she went, she turned round and said, 'Is it about Zarok?' Gavin's face went white and pinched. The others groaned or put their heads in their hands...

'Whaaah??' went Reubin, as if to suggest that Gavin had told her.

'Go away now, Billie. No it's not!' replied Gavin hotly, widening his eyes at his friends.

'What does she know?' hissed Greg. 'She sussed it Drew?'

'That's the last thing we need!' said Raj, looking the most concerned. Shocked, in fact.

'Don't worry! I'll find out later. Let's jus' get on with our meeting!' But seconds later, the boys' mum burst through the door. It wasn't all bad; she held a tray which was wobbling with mugs of steaming hot chocolate. Greg ran to hold the door open properly for her.

'Thank you!' they all said apart from Terry who said, 'Nice one!'

'I wasn't exactly sure of numbers… How come your new friend you've been going around with isn't here with you?' asked Miriam with a raised (perfectly plucked) eyebrow.

'Eh?' said Gavin by way of a response.

'The one who wears sunglasses in the winter?' she pressed, wiping some spills from her apron. At this, Terry stifled a peel of laughter down his jumper, turning it into a snort.

'I haven't got a new friend. It must be Xavier's half-brother, he wears sunnies!'

'But I know Xavier's mum. He hasn't got a half-brother!'

'Oh yeah… I mean Jake's,' Gavin added quickly, hoping he'd come up with someone whose mum she didn't know.

'Oh! Alright then' said Miriam, leaving the room.

'Phew!' said Drew. 'It's getting harder innit?'

'You mean to hide him like! It must be!' agreed Terry, who was at last looking more concerned.

'Down to business!' cut in Drew. 'How do we make sure Terry n' Greg can definitely get on our group trip!'

'Let's just take it as it comes!' suggested Reubin, slurping his hot chocolate as noisily as possible. He was right. They didn't need to worry. The boys soon slipped up to Gavin and Drew's room to see Zarok. They had been dying to see him, yet their football practise had been suffering. Once they'd fought for the best seat on the bed, the friends filled Zarok in on all of the USA Presentation Projects, with their typical boisterousness and digressions. As Zarok lay down on the bottom of Drew's bunk bed, he took it all in delightedly. All in all, it had turned out to be such a normal, yet utterly enjoyable afternoon. He knew in his heart that there would not be many such Saturdays left like it…

***

A couple of days passed uneventfully, which in reality was best for the boys. But now it was midweek and the pupils of Higglesdon Wick first year (and Juniors) were dying to hear the results of their presentations. Luckily, they did not have long to wait. It was before lunch, just ten minutes into Anderson's geography lesson when Mr Baldwin strolled in wearing a smart chequered suit.

'Shhh!!!' admonished the pupils to each other, not wanting to fail at the last hurdle.

'Good Morning everyone!' said Mr Baldwin, addressing the class.

'Good Morning Mr Baldwin!' came the reply from Gavin's class in unison, sounding less bored than usual.

'I decided to address you class by class rather than have another long assembly.'

'But he always goes on long whatever!' hissed Raj to Gavin, who elbowed him.

'A tradition of ours in assembly, as you know, has been to select up to three pupils a week to reward them for 'stand out' deeds. This can range from excellent work or behaviour, to punctuality, meritorious deeds or a marked improvement! We are aware that Montgomery, Dan, Xavier or Raj are top of the class. However, today I am gratified to select Gavin for this week's reward for what can only be described as outstanding homework.' He held out a hand to Gavin who ran up the aisle to (clumsily) shake it.

'This means you may take one afternoon off as you please, Gavin, or request a special favour, within reason, from your form tutor!' The class dutifully clapped but they so wanted Mr Baldwin to get to the USA bit! Mr Baldwin now shook a handful of forms at the confused class.

'In all of these USA forms, few of you have written down a second attraction, US State or destination. I'm afraid this has affected our choice as to where to place all our pupils, even if it has made a hard job easier. A dedicated panel of teachers has been committed to making this selection process as good as it can be! Some of you may be very upset initially, which is why we do not want scenes in assembly, plus you can put your questions to me right here with your class support!' Mr Baldwin did not alter his tone much and it was making the pupils rather restless, or even sleepy.

'Get on with it mate…' whispered Gavin to Lee.

'I see little evidence of 'Special Needs' on the forms. The special needs are not something to be embarrassed about, but are designed to help you. I want you to take your forms back to your parents and have them check them again. With regards to going abroad, this need not be about help with learning, such as dyslexia. It may be that you have special dietary requirements, need to take medication or have considerations that you and ourselves need to take into account as part of your beliefs. We want you to be able to fit in your normal needs and routines alongside our trip.' Mr Baldwin expanded on both needs and special needs for the trip… but he'd mostly lost their attention. In fact, he went on and on…

But they perked up when he said: 'Now for the results!' He then stroked his moustache thoughtfully for a moment before starting again.

'I'm afraid some of the girls here are going to be disappointed. Chloe's team in the other class clinched the skiing…'

'Ohhh!! Why can't we go too! Please, can't we go with them!' Melissa and Ife burst out, hopelessly unable to contain their disappointment. Mr Baldwin sighed.

'Their presentation was the better of the two on this occasion. Not only that, we have created a group that will not only do a week's skiing, but will also embark on quite a strenuous outdoor adventure holiday that involves trekking in harsh terrain, kayaking and allsorts. It's not for the faint-hearted! I'm reliably informed that hiking turns around the behaviour of those who have displayed less than model behaviour, so we need places for such pupils. The rest of them are keen, young sports people.'

'So are we!' cried Bethany indignantly. Mr Baldwin moved on with a sickly grin.

'That's one out of four destinations…The next is as follows: New York!'

'Like we couldn't have guessed,' muttered Gideon crossly to his pals.

'A bulk of the pupils will be visiting New York. It's not just that the group put on a great show, New York has a lot to offer and is easy to negotiate for the purpose of school trips! They can go to Staten Island and all sorts. It will be a lot of fun. I think a couple of you in this class may have chosen New York as a second choice; so you may consult the list afterwards and see if you were picked.'

The children were getting worried now. The choices were thin on the ground with only two left. *What were the chances of California or Miami?* thought Gideon's gang, looking poker-faced now. But Gavin's friends hadn't given up hope at all.

'It ain't over til' it's over…' whispered Reubin philosophically.

'Yeah bruv… Up yer game Baldy,' Gavin whispered back to a now spluttering and smirking Reubin.

'The third choice…' boomed Mr Baldwin majestically, 'Is…Disneyland!' Now the girls who had chosen Disneyland went wild with excitement.

'Yeaaarghhhh! Aaarrgh!!! We're goin' to Disneyworld!' screamed Sian and Verity, going over to shake Belinda and Rowena whilst caterwauling with laughter.

'WE WON! We're going!!!' DISNEY! DISNEY! DISNEY!' they screeched.

Mr Baldwin covered his eardrums, looking in pain now. 'Alright, Alright! Good! After much consideration it was decided that Disneyland was such a popular choice that we couldn't forgo it. Pupils and teachers alike managed to persuade me that it was educational on a fair number of accounts. Naturally, any of you who go, if at all, will be accompanied by many of the juniors. We have our final choice coming. This is, in fact, the most significant choice for the bulk of you in this class. Now, bearing in mind that your wonderful geography teacher doubles up as your form tutor, I think it would be most beneficial to take advantage of this…' Gavin was poised now to spring into the air. *What he wanted to hear had to be coming…*

'So Class 1G…CALIFORNIA…' The class erupted into shouts, squeals and screams of rapture. Beside himself, Gideon leapt six feet off his chair into the air…Baldwin was also getting beside himself now, getting distracted, cross and mopping a hankie to his brow.

'Sit down and be quiet! Immediately!' he ordered. 'Or none of you will be going anywhere apart from outside my office!' The children puckered up and shut up!

'CALIFORNIA or MIAMI did NOT make it into the final selection this time!

Your USA destination will be ARIZONA!' It was now Gavin's turn to leap six feet in the air out of his chair, and the next thing all his pals were joining him, doing what they considered to be a kind of bear dance in the middle of the room! They were ecstatic!

'WE DID IT!' shouted Gavin. 'ARIZONA ALL the WHA-HAY!!!' And then came the football chants and whoops and shouts of joy! And despite themselves, all of his class joined in, both for him and themselves…All apart from Gideon and Diggory, Montgomery and Josh who remained seated and utterly defeated! Bang had gone Miami and their dreams with it. You had to feel a bit sorry for them. Not only that, it was another battle lost and another battle won to their bitter rivals. Mr Baldwin was anxious to leave, what with all the commotion, but his parting piece was…

'I think you will have a wonderful time in Arizona! The slide show was most inspiring and the Grand Canyon will make you appreciate the wonders of nature! Indeed, the description of the Coronado Scenic Byway that was mentioned during Gavin's group presentation sounded a very nice addition to the trip to my mind. Please view the lists outside your classroom or school noticeboard to see who will be going and to make sure your name is indeed on the list. And that will be all. It's all yours, Mr Anderson!' And with that, Mr Baldwin swept out.

But there was one more thing that Gavin wished to clinch before the lesson was over.

'You know I may suggest a reward, Mr Anderson.'

'Yes Gavin.'

'I'd like to choose Terry n' Greg to accompany us to Arizona. They are my friends in the juniors…'

'I will speak to their tutors Gavin, and if that is what they want and both parties agreeable, I see no reason why not!'

'At least we can gamble in Las Vegas…' Josh consoled Gideon, who looked like he was about to lash out at someone. But that cheered him up.

***

Gavin couldn't wait to get out of school and race home to tell Zarok the news. Raj had texted Drew before even Gavin, so Drew felt the same way. He was waiting for his brother outside the school gates at 3.30am and the pair, along with Reubin, tore up the road, running nearly all the way. It helped them to cope with the excitement. Once in, they threw themselves on Zarok, pummelling him as they joyously shouted out the good news.

'You've done amazing Gavin…You really did that? I mean… dudes! It's crazy!' Zarok sat up on the bed, trying to get his breath back. His eyes were shining and he was smiling the most beatific smile. But for him, it was mixed feelings. It would mean that soon he would have to leave the Masons. He was happy there…Yet he didn't want to die there. The next step was necessary.

'I can't believe it, Gavin! Can you Drew? But…But…Tell me how can I go with you? We realised that me going to your school all turned out a bit of a disaster!' The boys hesitated, looking sombre for a moment. They weren't too keen on sorting out logistics right at that moment.

'Hey Zarok! We will celebrate with some soda pop…And then we'll talk about it!' Drew came back with four cold soda pops and straws in a bottle.

'Easy! We'll put him in a suitcase,' said Reubin simply.

'We will have to adapt it- with air holes' added Drew, liking the plan.

'Sounds like a plan!' said Gavin who fled the room to go look for one right away. Now was as good a time as any to see if Zarok could fit in one.

Ten minutes later and Gavin had found one in the corner of their loft. It was one of the ones that you could wheel along. They were glad Lee wasn't there to ask such questions as 'what if airport security look at it?' They would have to cross each bridge as they came to it. Zarok was small and curled upright in the suitcase with his knees tight against his chest. Then Drew slowly zipped it around him.

'How does that feel Zarok?'

'It's OK!' came the muffled reply. 'I'll need some airholes though!' Once out, Zarok explained to them how his breathing was 'extra sensitive' in a good way.

'I can breathe well through pores in my body as I'm made with special capacities in that way. I'm far less likely than you to overheat; plus I can go without water longer… and food.'

'That's just as well then! Thank goodness for that!' said Drew relieved.

'You sure?!' quizzed Gavin.

'I am able to sort of hibernate. You know how animals do? What happens is, that I can slow my metabolism right down at will. So I am confident that I could make the trip!'

'As long as we don't get caught!' groaned Reubin. 'Tis risky yana?!'

'But Gavin, Drew!' remembered Zarok.

'It's your trip too! What about clothes and all the stuff you will need to take?' Reubin enlightened them now.

'Yeah! You may only take a certain amount of weight on a trip.'

'Do you? Well I don't need anything, apart from the clothes I stand up in, and neither does Drew!' Drew, who was already foraging for his binoculars, looked about to differ, but he kept silent. Gavin, who read him, said: 'We've got no choice, have we? Zarok is the most important consideration here! That's why we are goin' to Arizona! Who needs a stupid ole bar of soap or binoculars Drew?!'

'Or clean jeans or pants or a raincoat!' reminded Reubin, who liked wearing a nice pair of jeans, even more so on a trip abroad. So he changed his mind, saying: 'Mind I do want mi get up. Gotta tink of mi look yana dups?'

'We will wear three pairs of pants on the day! And take one really good outfit!' stated Gavin undeterred.

'We can wash 'em every day!' said Drew.

'You can, I won't!' decided Gavin. Then Zarok came in.

'What you could do is take a decent-sized day bag. You can take that with you on the coach and everywhere, but fill it with other things you need. Perhaps Lee, Raj, Greg and Terry can take big day bags too and put a few of your things in them?' Zarok was back out of the case now, inspecting it.

'Yeah! They can coz I won't!' stated Reubin firmly. He wanted to take as much as he could, yet travel light as well.

'Shut up Reubin! Thanks Zarok, that's a really good idea. I'm sure Terry 'n Greg won't mind!' said Gavin, glaring at Reubin. Then Gavin changed tack.

'Gosh! Think of it Reubs! We're goin' to Las freakin' Vegas! With all of our mates! We're going to have such a brilliant time!'

'And in February! Missing school! Yay! Arizona here we come! Maad!'

And that was that. Bit by bit, the boys were getting organised and sorted. Over the next few weeks, more considerations were brought up and grappled with. Miriam bought her sons nice, practical waterproofs and new boots. They had saved up every penny of their pocket money. Everything was going according to plan, so nothing could go wrong now, could it?

***

They were due to go on February the eighth, depending on the weather. Lee had approached the boys with a nice idea. That was for all of them to go and eat in his family's restaurant with their mums and dads. The idea had gone down well. So the week before they were to leave, a party arrived there. It consisted of Gavin, Drew, Billie, Miriam and Brian. Reubin came with his mum Honour and her husband, and then there was Terry with his dad, Raj with his dad and Greg with his guardian, Mildred. Lee's family had their own family celebration that evening and they all gathered in one area. Red lanterns and paper cuttings adorned that corner and even a door God. All were flushed and excited, not just because of the party, but because the restaurant was the talk of the town! Being no ordinary Chinese restaurant, it served up modern takes on the menu with fashionable fusions.

The restaurant sparkled as it swept around in a curvaceous expanse, so that groups of diners could enjoy an intimate setting. There were lotus flowers on ponds and orchids and pretty lighting that glowed incandescently.

'I didn't know you had a big family, Lee?' exclaimed Miriam, looking well dressed in an azure silk dress.

'Yes, I do!' he grinned. 'It's good because they are all here or at home. You see we had Chinese New Year recently. We call it Shou Sui.'

'What's traditional Lee?'

'Oh you know, fireworks, fish and dumplings at home...' (Lee clocked Terry n' Greg doing a fake yawn. They would rather have done this minus the folks.)

'Oh yes! I understand you have a family reunion dinner for that, and don't you stay awake all night?' asked Honour, wondering why they were still there.

Lee grinned, noting her slightly uncertain expression.

'Yep! They've been there ever since! Our New Year lasts for fifteen days! Yuan Xiao festival is the end of the New Year celebrations.'

'Mercy! So they are not outstaying their welcome!' she laughed. 'Lucky I didn't suggest that you do as we do in our culture; put a broom upside down in the corner of the yard when they do!'

'Some of them are,' replied Lee confidentially. 'But it's good on the whole as I get to say goodbye to them before the trip. Two of them gave me a red envelope with money in it too,' he smiled triumphantly. (The boys gave him a knowing, appreciative nod at this revelation.)

'Do you like cooking, Lee? Gavin's mother and I love to cook!' said Honour.

'No!' answered Lee bluntly, looking sheepish. 'I just like eating it! But my older brother is a really good chef! It's many of his ideas that have brought this place on trend!'

'Ooh! That sounds very good, Lee! We are so looking forward to it!' gushed the ladies. (Terry's dad, however, would have preferred fish and chips.) They happily ordered a medley of dishes served in coconut bowls. Despite the poshness of the affair, Gavin and his mates put it all away ravenously, hardly communicating. That's how they enjoyed their food the most! Yet afterwards, there was much fun and conversation during the sweet and over lychee granitas with lemongrass biscuits and creamy silky soya panacottas with edible flowers. Supper went down a treat!

'Ant's follow fat, fat drown im!' joked Honour's rotund husband Barrington which meant that excessive greed will hurt you! (The children laughed long and loud at this.) It appeared the whole affair was on the house, though when Lee's dad came over to chat to the adults, the families wouldn't hear of it. They didn't turn down a healthy discount, however! Lee's mum soon appeared beside him wishing them 'Xinnian Hao' and 'Shenti Jiankang'! This meant 'Happy New Year' and 'Enjoy good health'. 'Traditional' she twinkled, leaving some treats wrapped in serviettes on the table. They were sweet dumplings or tangyuan, which were sweet dumplings, particular to Yuan Xiao. Lee was really chuffed to share hospitality with his friends, and they were all most grateful and happy.

The occasion settled everyone and helped them to set their sights upon the trip. It would be the last 'hurrah'; a lovely chance for the families to discuss the USA trip and enjoy quality time together before the final preparations, and a long period of not seeing their children – for ten days at the least! And with that, the well-fed party made their way into the main street, so that they could keep Terry and his dad and Greg and his guardian Mildred, company at the bus stop. It was raining, so Honour's husband kept them all dry, thanks to his golf umbrella, while Miriam had brought umbrellas for herself and the boys, which embarrassed them!

'Since it's got dark, it is good of you to keep us company at the bus stop!' beamed Terry's dad, secretly wondering why a lift hadn't been offered.

'Could be a long wait too!' added Mildred, gaping into the street that was empty of buses. Gavin and Drew scanned the timetable for bus times while the adults engaged in chit-chat, before turning to view a poster plastered on the bus shelter, which left them in open-mouthed horror… Terry had noticed it first and nudged Reubin urgently.

'Sh…indigs!' he yelled, saving the obvious expletive in time.

'Reubin!' scolded Honour. 'Don't be uncouth!' But Reubin was deaf to his mum, watching on as friends Gavin and Drew went deathly pale.

There was no mistaking it. The poster, although rather blurred and presumably taken from CCTV footage, was of none other than Zarok! Sure he was wearing his sunglasses and hoodie, but his strange little mouth and pinched flat nostrils gave him away.

'Good grief! That looks like the kid you boys were with at your gig! The one who always wears sunglasses!' exclaimed Honour, pursing her lips at Miriam. 'I knew he looked no good!'

The poster read: *'On Friday 13th of January, a youth reported to be about ten years old committed a theft on Higglesdon Wick High Street in Gresham Stores & Supplies. The youth, as identified from CCTV footage, made off with supplies of sweet potatoes, molasses, blueberry soda and a number of small cactus plants. This was an unprovoked attack upon the owner's goods and sense of safety and security. We believe this brazen youth presents a serious, potential nuisance to our hometown! Anyone with any information upon this matter, please contact Higglesdon Wick Police Station where your information will be treated in confidence. Reward offered!*

'Poor Mr Gresham and his wife! Lord have mercy! Think I might pop into the police station myself and say I've witnessed the young man!' cried Honour, looking shocked.

'Witnessed the blighter?!' suggested Miriam. But Miriam was glaring at her boys who were trying not to meet her gaze.

'Sweet potatoes and molasses and cactus, aye? Well, that is a coincidence to be sure!'

'Oh honestly!' gasped Brian exasperated. 'Doing a number… Well I be scundered!' And embarrassed he was in front of everyone.

'I've told you already! There's a craze for making homemade clocks out of organic matter! Not everyone can afford the materials, can they Greg?'

'Really? Really Gavin?' pressed Miriam. Her eyes widened so much they looked as if they would pop out of her head now. Her greeny-blue eyeshadow, instead of enhancing her, now made his mum look downright evil, thought Drew.

'Hear me Miriam, dem say, 'Bad ting neva got owner!' declared Honour, casting a sparky eye at her boys. She meant that no one wants to take responsibility for a bad situation.

'We have had such a lovely evening. Let us not spoil it,' suggested Mildred shyly.

'Pickney dem!' vocalised Honour, sharing a knowing look with Miriam.

'Cockroach neva right before chicken,' mumbled Reubin reproachfully to his mum. He knew, she knew, that it meant that one will never be judged fairly by one's enemies… It was something she would say, after all.

'Whaah?' cried Honour, grabbing hold of her husband who looked baffled and sleepy after the abundant meal. Yet Reubin and Gavin knew a hasty retreat was called for! The longer they stayed, the more they would get rumbled.

'Phew! Saved by the bus!' whooped Raj tactlessly, as he and his dad made a move in the other direction, anxious to go home now. And sure enough, the red bus, which was never more of a welcome sight, trundled into view. With that, Terry, his dad, Greg and Mildred got on. Then, in a flash of inspiration, so did Drew, Gavin and Reubin! Hopping on, they were relieved to be leaving their parents to walk back to the car and take themselves home without them!

'Phew!' demonstrated Drew as Terry's dad chuckled softly. He found the latest affair rather amusing and wanted to help them out.

'You and Drew can come and stay over with Terry tonight if that would help?' he offered smiling.

'Yeah, you don't know the ole boy an' the ole girl!' griped Gavin. 'It would make it even worse. Better go home and face the music. Alright then… Can we stay for an hour like?'

'What about me!' burst out Reubin. So all the boys stayed at Terry's for an hour, with the football on the widescreen in the background.

'A freakin' poster demanding a reward for him!' raged Drew, more alarmed than ever.

'The show is over!' came back Terry grimly, pretending to slice his neck.

'It's all gonna come out now!'

'I mean a freakin' 'Wanted Reward' poster for Zarok! And they'll bare be all over the town – like a rash! *Lond up dil ting big time!*' he added for effect, which meant that Zarok's business would be disclosed massively. 'What about when Gideon's gang see it, and Baldy an' that other head, Herbert! Oh *zeen...*' Reubin elaborated, getting the measure of it. Meanwhile, Terry and Greg were updating Raj and Lee by text.

'DON'T!' yelled Reubin. 'Ejjits! The FBI will be on to us. They can investigate texts! The long arm of the law will be on to us, you know!'

'It will have to be a very long arm then, because we'll be in America!' quipped Terry, carelessly relaxing back on the sofa.

'*Have to be a very long arm of the law coz we'll be in America!*' shrieked Gavin and Reubin appreciatively. They liked Terry's joke and kept repeating it over and over for a while, falling all over each other as they creased up with laughter imagining an arm as long as that.

'You got bare jokes Tez-face!'

'Yeah an' don't I know it!' boasted Terry. 'Skill!' he added, as if he'd scored a goal. Then the three of them hi-fived and rubbed Terry's head affectionately.

Despite their misgivings, he'd been fine over Zarok. He was his own person, more of a leader than a follower really, and that was why. He could also be insensitive, but it was all good now. The boys felt a bit better now after a belly laugh.

'Yeah! It's just as well that we're going on our trip now!' laughed Drew. 'He'll be gone with us! And that will be the end of it...' The boys paused for thought, slightly mollified.

'Hear mi! Do road! That's what we say to go on an outing like a trip.'

'I like that, 'Do road' sounds cool Reubs,' acknowledged Drew.

'Anyways, I reckon you better get home then after your tea dups,' suggested Reubin.

'What if they go looking for him in your room or garage?'

Gavin and Drew looked at each other aghast. 'Aarghh!' they cried in unison. They supped up and shot out of Terry's, just about remembering to shout 'goodbye! And 'thank you!' The boys fled all the way home.

'It's true Drew. This is going to go downhill all the way, but as you say, we *are* going away. So we mustn't panic. We just gotta get Zarok out of here!' On the way home, the brothers were horrified to find three 'Wanted Reward' posters featuring Zarok. Yes, right on their own doorstep!

Once the boys were home, Miriam was a bit softer on them.

'You are wet through boys! Hot baths and straight to bed or you'll get a cold and that will be no good for your trip.' The boys decided to say nothing and did just that. But before they each took a bath, they noticed a dim light on in the shed from their bedroom. Drew flashed his mobile at the window three times, and Zarok flashed back. The message meant, come up and see us when the coast is clear. At least for now, our plucky Black Eyed Kid remained safe and sound in the boy's garden shed, still in hiding. But while our intrepid Dogs of Hell slept soundly, more posters were being printed for the purposes of being plastered up all over Higglesdon Wick... They were, of course, the ones that concerned Zarok, and they painted a heinous picture of him! They were the posters inviting all of the town's people to come and give information about him! Overnight, Zarok had become a criminal and a fugitive with a **'WANTED REWARD'** sign over his head!

To be continued…

MINI URBAN GLOSSARY FOR ADEKCTS

A who you man? – What are you up to/Who are you really?

Bare – Emphasis; whether good, bad, a lot

Beat dem bad – Surpass them/Be better than them

Beef – Trouble

Big man – Famous person

Big tings – Big things/Monetary success

Big ups – Credit to

Blud – Friend

Bossman – One in charge

Breathe easy – Calm down

Bruv – Friend/Brother

Crawb up – Looking good/Something good

Creps – Shoes

Dat Shot! – That's fantastic; used to describe something fabulous

Dem – Them

Do road – Go on an outing

Do yu ting – Go ahead, do your thing

Don't get mi ig – Don't get me upset

Donk – An idiot

Dope – Wicked, cool!

Dups/Doops – Friend

Eejit – An idiot

Endz – Neighbourhod

G'waan – What's going on?/How are you?

Get up – One's outfit

Knock mi – Call me/text me

Level – Calm down

Likkle more – See you later

Live a luu – Spoil the plan

Lon dil ting – Long deal thing/Something that will be a big
    deal or go on

Lond up dil ting – Disclose someone's business

Maad! – Awesome

Memba mi tell yu – Listen up mate

Neek – Geek

One more time – A term to indicate the extreme

OT – Out of town

Pickney dem – Them kids

Po po – Police

Pompasetting – Showing off

Popping – Active, happening

Pree – Check out

Safe – OK, all good

Shell dun/Shell dung – Do something fantastic

Spit – To rap

Turn up! – Turn it up/Bring it!

Wah gwaan – What's going on?

Wassy – Weird

Waste man – Useless person

Yana – You know

Zeen/Oh zeen! – You understand/Oh yes

Hi readers,

I am an indie writer. If you enjoyed this book, please show your support and write me a review on Amazon. This will help me to get the sequel out to you in good time.

Many thanks!
Karine

www.ingramcontent.com/pod-product-compliance
Lightning Source LLC
Chambersburg PA
CBHW050355190726
48284CB00007BB/2288